Mystery at the Fair

A Jean Hays Story
Book 1

Connie Cockrell

ISBN: 13:978-1515050490
ISBN: 10:1515050491

DEDICATION

To all of the family, friends, and acquaintances who
encouraged me to try my hand at something new.

OTHER BOOKS BY CONNIE COCKRELL

The Bad Seed

Trio of Animal Tales

Recall

Halloween Tales: A Collection of Stories

Christmas Tales

Gulliver Station Stories
A New Start
The Challenge
Hard Choices
Revolution

Brown Rain Series
The Beginning
The Downtrodden

Jean Hays Series
Mystery at the Fair
Mystery in the Woods

ACKNOWLEDGMENTS

To my friends at Forward Motion
(http://www.fmwriters.com) and Power Writing Hour for
their support. To EJ at Silver Jay Media for being such a
patient and supportive editor.

CHAPTER ONE

Jean Hays trudged across the fairgrounds. Sweat dripped down her temples. The sun beat down out of a cornflower-blue sky while end-of-the-monsoon season thunderheads built up into towering blinding white and ominous portents of future rain. *Wish I'd remembered my hat. That's what I get. March had seemed so pleasant. Who knew September would mimic an oven with misters?*

She reached the first of two shipping containers the Hise County Fair used as storage lockers. They called them Conex boxes. Jean remembered seeing them on every Air Force base she'd ever been on. She glanced at the cloud studded sky. Rain every year for the fair, she'd heard the Exhibits team say before she'd trudged to the storage container where the plastic tubs of left over ribbons, banners and other fair paraphernalia resided the rest of the year. She wiped her face and hoped the units were unlocked. The Fair Board President, Arris Van Horn wasn't answering his phone. *I hope Arris came by and unlocked these. He should have them open by now.* Jean examined the two-part mechanism to open the container. She briefly touched the handles. The doors received full sun all day. They were hot but not hot enough to give a burn. Jean pulled on one lever. Part of the mechanism moved a rod that connected with a top and bottom notch but it didn't allow the door to open. She wiped the sweat from her forehead. *I really need to learn to wear a hat.*

Jean had moved to Greyson, Arizona in February. It had been winter—there was even a bit of snow. Old northeastern habits died hard, she never used to wear a hat. Now, though, she wished for her wide-brim hiking hat to give her some relief. *Must be ninety degrees out here.*

She tried the second handle on the door. It lifted another bar. Maybe both of them at the same time? Jean lifted them both. The vertical bars lifted and lowered, freeing the door. She tugged it open. *Now I don't have to track Arris down.* He had the keys and the combinations to every lock and door on the fairgrounds. Jean was totally dependent on his expertise. She hadn't been VP of Exhibits more than four months so she was still learning how things worked in this county.

She swung the container doors open wide. The doorway was a tangled mess of everything the fairgrounds needed to have stored. Jean pulled a wooden tripod out of the doorway and used it to prop the right-hand door open. It looked as though it was a sign post. A lot of other events that were held at the fairgrounds used these containers. Five feet into the container she wished she'd brought a flashlight. Sweat began dripping in earnest as she peered into the musty darkness. *Smells like mice in here. Hope they haven't gotten into the tubs.*

Winding her way past safety cones, stacked tables, buckets of rope, steel cable and broken metal chairs, she stepped over a pile of rebar to reach her stack of tubs. One, two, three, four, she counted. *Where's the fifth tub?* The heat was giving her a headache so she massaged her temples after she'd wiped her filthy hands on her shorts. She hauled the bins out to the front of the container. When those were outside she decided to check farther to the back. The Exhibits team had been sure there ought to be five bins. A pile of cardboard boxes labeled *Mud Run* blocked her way. Jean moved the three boxes behind her and stepped over a pile of rusting chain. *It's creepy and dirty in here. Let me just find the box and get out.*

Squinting, she saw a medium blue tub labeled Fair Ribbons out of reach on top of another stack of bins. *There you are.* She wiped her face again and held her breath. The smell of dead things was overwhelming. I hope nothing crawled into my bin. The ribbons will be ruined. She picked her way past boxes, rusting metal things she couldn't identify and a broken ladder. She pulled the tilted bin toward her—just a little more—and then the whole pile of bins fell over with a godawful racket. Her bin slid to the floor, taking part of her thumbnail with it and raising a cloud of dust.

"Owww!" she cried as she jerked her hand away and stuck the injured digit in her mouth. In front of her, the two doors of a metal cabinet against the right-hand wall of the container creaked open and a desiccated human body fell out of it in seeming slow motion.

In the moments it fell, her eyes were wide as her brain tried to make sense of the situation; she could see long hair trailing behind the head as the thing toppled. Female, was her instant thought, especially as the body wore a woman's pink down vest. The vest was discolored with rust stains. Then Jean realized that the discoloration must be body fluids. Her stomach rolled and as the thing hit the bin at her feet, she shrieked and scrambled outside.

Panting, she stared at the gaping mouth of the container. Jean pulled her cell phone out of her pocket and dialed 911. When the operator answered she said, "This is Jean Hays, VP of Exhibits at the fairgrounds. I just found a dead body in the storage container on the southwest side of the grounds."

CHAPTER TWO

Standing inside the yellow crime scene tape next to an ambulance, Jean watched what looked like complete chaos as an EMT bandaged her thumb.

"That should do it." He smoothed the tape. "You should get a tetanus shot, too. The Emergency Care place over on the corner of the highway and Longview Street can take care of you. If you go to the hospital emergency room it'll cost more."

"Thanks." Jean examined her thumb. "I'll do that." She nodded toward the crowd of milling police, the coroner and EMTs. "Crime scenes always look like this?"

He shrugged. "Don't know. There hasn't been a murder in town since I started working eleven years ago."

They were interrupted by a uniformed officer. "Who said it was a murder?" He was about six foot, wearing a tan uniform over a well-muscled body. This guy didn't sit around drinking coffee and eating donuts. He was clean shaven with a chiseled face, all planes and cheekbones. The dark blue eyes under bushy brows looked as though they didn't miss much. Fancy insignia marched along the shirt's shoulder epaulets. He had cowboy boots on his feet. They seemed incongruous to her.

"It looked like a murder to me." Jean nodded her thanks to the EMT who gave her a wink and left. The officer's tone annoyed her. She held out her right hand. "I'm Jean Hays."

He shook her hand after a brief look of suspicion. "I'm Chief of Police Nick White. You found the body?"

"Scared the crap out of me. Fell out of the double door cabinet. Stuff was piled in front of it that held the doors closed. If it was a suicide, how'd stuff get piled in front of the door?" She jerked her chin at the small crowd gathering outside the tape. "The press is here."

Chief White turned to see a photographer taking pictures with a long lens. "That's Scott Duley, works for the town newspaper. The editor will be calling me soon for the story." He turned back to her. "Did you recognize the body?"

"No." Jean was hot and wanted a drink of water. A whole bottle of icy cold water sounded really good, what with the sun beating down on her head. "Not really. I mean, I think it was female, long hair and a pink jacket, but it was too dark in there and I was busy getting out. I've only lived here a few months, anyway. Most people are still strangers."

His left eyebrow cocked up. "A newcomer? You're on the Fair Board. How'd that happen?"

Jean shrugged. His tone indicated he didn't think much of new residents. "Not hard. They needed volunteers and I'm a good organizer."

Nick eyed her. "You have the keys to the Conex?" He studied her reaction.

She shook her head. "Sorry, Chief, I don't. Arris Van Horn holds the keys."

"So the box was just open?" He adjusted his equipment belt, then the cowboy hat.

It was Jean's turn to raise an eyebrow. "Sure. We're setting up the fair. Volunteers are in and out of this thing all day." She furrowed her brow. "You think Arris did this? A poor place to hide a body, since he's in charge of the container."

The Chief sniffed. "It's a small town and I've lived here all my life, as has Arris. As to whether Arris did it, I don't know, maybe." He looked around and waved an officer over. "Take Ms. Hays's statement and let her get back to her business."

"What about my bins?"

"Sorry, we'll have to take them to the lab. They're part of the evidence." He didn't even look at her, just turned and walked to the gurney where the body lay covered.

CHAPTER THREE

Jean finished giving her statement, then stomped back to the Exhibits building. She was hot and thirsty and her thumb hurt. The doors to the building were open, letting in light and air but there was no air conditioning. She went straight to the cooler she'd brought this morning for the volunteers. It was full of bottles of water on ice. She grabbed one, twisted the cap off and started gulping it down. The water was so cold it made her teeth hurt and gave her instant brain freeze. She winced and pressed her hand to her forehead.

She heard a laugh behind her. "You shouldn't drink it so fast. You'll have a stroke or something."

Jean turned around. It was her new friend, Karen Carver, the Superintendent of Homemaking Arts. Karen was grinning, her blue-gray eyes crinkled in the corners. A smudge of dirt ran from her cheek to her chin and her blond hair was coming loose from her pony-tail. It fell in wisps all around her face. "I'm so thirsty." She held the cold water bottle to her temple.

"I stood around out there in the sun for over an hour."

"You should get a hat."

"Tell me about it." Jean sipped some more of the water. "And I ripped half my thumbnail off." She held the bandaged thumb up for Karen to see.

"Did you find the bins?"

Jean moved aside as two men carried a display case past. "Thought we'd try putting the case in the center of the floor," the tall, gray-haired one of the two said. John Gonzales was the Superintendent of Gems and Minerals, and had been with the fair in that role for decades. "Seems like people just walk down the middle of the room and never look at what's displayed on the sides."

"Sounds like a plan, John. Go ahead and try that. We just need to be sure there's four feet of space all around it, otherwise the Fire Marshal will make us move it."

"Sure, I'll make sure."

She and Karen watched them carry the case another twenty feet and set it down. Sounds of hammering, people chatting and discussing display arrangements filled the warehouse-sized building. Lucky for Jean all of the Superintendents had been doing this for years. They didn't need her to tell them how to set up. She sat down on the cooler lid and finished the water.

"So what happened out there?" Karen tried to smooth all of the wisps of hair back out of her face.

"Well. After I found four of them, I spotted the last bin on top of a wobbly stack of boxes in front of a two door cabinet. I pulled it toward me and the whole stack toppled over. The bin took a chunk of my nail. While I was nursing that, the cabinet doors creaked open and this dried-up old body fell out."

Karen gasped, hand over mouth. "So that's what all the commotion was about. I wondered about all the cop cars. When I saw the ambulance I figured someone in Livestock got hurt."

"Scared the crap out of me. I shrieked like a little girl and ran out of the container. I'm lucky I didn't skewer myself on some rusty piece of junk that's piled in there."

"I'd have screamed, too." Karen shook her head. "Then what?"

"I called 911. The first cop car showed up in just a few minutes. Then it was a zoo—ambulances, more police cruisers, then gawkers. I saw the photographer from the paper trying to get pics from outside the crime scene tape." Jean got up and pulled another bottle of water out of the cooler. She sipped it this time. "I'm still dehydrated. And I'm supposed to get a tetanus shot, too."

"Go to the Emergency Care place."

"Yeah, that's what the EMT told me." She looked around at the activity.

"But what about the bins?"

"Oh!" Jean snorted. "They're being held as evidence. I asked the officer who took my statement how long they'd be held, and he said," she put on a drawl, "'I don't rightly know, ma'am. I s'pect the Chief would have a better idea.'" Jean rolled her eyes. "Good night. Do they teach them that drawl in cop school?"

Karen laughed. "I don't know. But we need those ribbons. What'll you do if we can't get them back from the cops?"

"When in danger or in doubt, run in circles, scream and shout."

Karen stared. "What?"

It was Jean's turn to laugh. "An old Air Force quote we used to say when it was hitting the fan and we had to improvise. I guess we'll think of something." She stood up, drained the bottle of water and dropped it in the trash bag she had next to the cooler. "Tell you what. I'll go get my shot and afterward I'll stop by the police station and see if I can't get an estimated time of release on the bins. Are you all okay here? Need me to get anything?"

Karen waved her off. "Go, get your shot. We'll be fine here. I'll ask around and see if any of the other Superintendents have ribbon ideas."

Jean grinned. "Thanks, you've got my cell number if you need anything while I'm gone."

As Jean drove to the Emergency Care office she thought about the Police Chief's insinuation about Arris. The man didn't strike her as a murderer. Months ago when she'd answered an article in the local paper, The Green Valley Gazette, she'd walked into the meeting at the high school Agricultural class room where the fair board meetings were held. A man at the front of the room had stood up. He had a sun-reddened face with bright blue eyes, tall, about six foot two, wearing jeans, a denim shirt, cowboy boots and a wide friendly grin, and there wasn't a creepy, killer-vibe about him. At the time she'd noted everyone else in the meeting room for the fair board was smiling, too.

When the board discussed whether to approve Jean as VP of Exhibits, Arris sat at the front of the room, waiting quietly for the group to come to a consensus. She'd liked that. It had shown a level of confidence and competence that had been quite reassuring.

Jean shook her head. If Arris was a killer then she was a ballerina. Jean put on her turn signal and pulled into the Emergency Care store-front parking lot. She turned off the engine and sighed. Her thumb throbbed. She decided that after the shot, she'd go home and swallow a couple of ibuprofen. There was no way she wanted to meet with that arrogant Police Chief without some pain killer in her system.

CHAPTER FOUR

The Police Station for Greyson was in a complex of other town buildings. There was plenty of parking for the Mayor's office, the town's Business Department, and the Water Department. They had solar panels over the parking lot here, too. She approved. It was Arizona, the town *should* be sucking every free dime of energy they could from a source that was available three hundred and forty or more days per year.

The front door of the Police Station led to a tiled hall. There was a small counter next to a window of bullet proof glass. At the window, green-tinted and with an annunciator in it, she saw an elderly woman typing on a computer. "Hi, I'm Jean Hays. I'd like to speak to Chief White concerning the incident at the fairgrounds this morning."

"I'll see if he's available." She picked up the handset of an office phone with multiple buttons running down the right side of the phone face. "Greta? The Chief in?" She listened for a moment. "A Ms. Hays to see the Chief about the murder."

So, word was already out. Jean shifted a little closer to the window to hear better.

"Yeah, I'll give her a visitor badge and send her in." She hung up and stood.

She's quick, Jean admitted as the woman wrote in a log and pulled a badge plainly labeled *Visitor* from a drawer. "Go to your left, I'll meet you at the door at the end of the hall."

Jean walked about twenty feet and found a door on her right. It only took a second for a buzzer to sound and the door to open. The woman was there and held out the badge. "Just clip it to your collar," she said, smiling. "Come on in."

Jean walked beside the woman through an office that could have been any business: government-issue desks, cheap office chairs, and people on phones or typing on computer keyboards. The only difference was that the people were mostly in police uniform and there were bars on the windows. "I expected some hard-boiled police officer at a high counter when I came in, to be honest."

The woman laughed. "Yeah, TV. Maybe that's because of the old stations back in New York City. I don't know if they still have it set up like that. We followed the current construction and layout advice for police stations when we built this station six years ago. Have to protect ourselves from the drug-addled and crazies out there." She opened an office door leading to a secretary. "By the way, I'm Martha, Ms. Hays. Greta will take good care of you." She nodded to the young woman inside as Jean stepped into the office. "You can lead her out afterward, Greta?"

"Sure, Martha. No trouble at all."

Martha closed the door behind Jean.

"Hello, Ms. Hays. The Chief is on the phone. Have a seat; he'll be done in a minute." She waved toward a row of chairs against the wall across from her desk.

"Thank you." Jean took a seat and picked up a magazine. *Sport and Field* she read on the tattered cover. The issue date was four years ago. She sighed and put the magazine down. Instead, she pulled a small notepad from her purse and began making a to-do list for the rest of the day and tomorrow. It nagged at her that the Chief suspected Arris could be the killer. She didn't know him that well but he didn't seem like the kind of man that went around killing people. But really, how many people did she know that were killers? What would a killer look like on normal days? Many a serial killer was supposedly very nice at his day job. What if Arris was like that? Nice until he was pissed off?

Her thoughts were interrupted by Greta. "The Chief can see you now, Ms. Hays."

Jean shook off the self-induced panic and stuffed her pen and pad back in her purse. "Thank you, Greta. Call me Jean."

Greta grinned and nodded as Jean stood and went to the inner office door where she knocked once. "Come in," came faintly through the solid oak door.

The doorknob turned easily. She found herself in an office that was all male. Police and Fire Department memorabilia covered the bookshelves and tables. Pictures of historic Greyson covered the walls. Nick stood up and motioned her to one of the two leather-covered chairs in front of his old fashioned wooden desk. "What can I do for you, Ms. Hays?"

He sat down as she did. "Chief, the reason I was in that storage container was to retrieve the fair's supply of ribbons for the exhibitors. I need those ribbons day after tomorrow for the judging of exhibits. Is there a time frame of when those bins might be released? I really need them."

The man's face looked as though he'd bitten into a sour grape. "Ms. Hays. I appreciate your predicament but it's going to take time to process the evidence we pulled from that container."

Jean was disappointed but she tried again. "I totally understand, Chief White." She sat a little more forward on the chair. "Would it be possible to dust them for prints, or whatever you have to do, first, so I can get them back?" *Come on*, she urged him mentally. *Give me a break, here.*

She could see his jaw working. *He isn't going to cut me any slack at all.*

"Ms. Hays, this isn't TV. We can't process evidence as fast as they show it on police shows. It takes time, and it's more than just dusting for fingerprints. The forensics expert needs time, and it's a one-person-deep office. I won't rush her."

Jean twisted her purse handles in her hands. His tone of voice indicated he thought she was out of line. All she could think about was how annoying he was and about how she was going to award ribbons to her exhibitors when they were all locked away in a lab somewhere. A mix of anger and panic washed over her. She stood up. "Sorry to take up so much of your valuable time." The words came out a bit snottier than she had meant. She could tell from the look on his face that she'd stepped over the line.

"Sorry I couldn't be of more help," he said, but the

words were cold and his eyes had narrowed.

She turned and left the office.

Greta looked up from her computer. "All done? That was fast." She stood up and came around the desk. "I'll walk you out."

"Thank you," Jean told her as she followed her out of the office, still miffed. "I appreciate your time."

Back in her car she fumed. "All he had to do was move my bins to the front of the line. The bins have nothing to do with the murder. Even if Arris's prints are on them, they're fair property. What would that even mean?" She smacked the steering wheel, then jammed the key into the ignition and started the car. *And what was I thinking? All I managed to do was sound like a shrew and ruin any chance he'd do me a favor. I'm such a moron.* She pulled out of the parking lot and headed back to the fairgrounds.

CHAPTER FIVE

When Jean arrived through the open double doors in the center of the Exhibits building, Karen was just starting to drape table skirts on her exhibit stands. "Hey, let me give you a hand." She grabbed another bottle of water from the cooler and walked over to the Homemaking Arts display area.

This building was different from the fair buildings where she'd exhibited as a 4-H member in upstate New York. Those had been barns, built in the 1800s. They didn't have air conditioning either but they had huge fans in the gables at either end of the building that sucked the hot, humid air of late summer upstate New York out of the building. It had always smelled of old wood and generations of 4-H kids who'd sweated and worked there. This building was just five years old. It had poured concrete floors, exhaust fans in the ceiling as well as at the gable ends and excellent overhead lighting. The pre-fab building even had toilets, which Jean was thankful for. Maybe next year she could wrangle air conditioning.

"How'd it go?" Karen pulled the thin clear plastic protector off of two feet of white plastic table-skirt glue edge.

"Terrible." Jean grabbed the other end of the twenty-foot-long skirting to make it easier for Karen to control sticking it to the stand. "The man is immovable. I explained that we need those ribbons for the day after tomorrow and he said he only had one crime lab tech and he wasn't going to rush her. I asked if the tubs could be processed first. He acted as though I was asking for the sacrifice of his firstborn child." She snorted with frustration. "I don't know what we're going to do for ribbons."

Karen laughed. "Yeah, Nick is kind of straight-laced. Even as a kid he always did things by the rules."

"He doesn't think much of newcomers either. I have the feeling he thinks I'm intruding. He was all over my being the VP of Exhibits this morning."

"Don't worry about him. Like most people born and raised here, he's seen a lot of changes in town since he was a boy. It has changed a lot. Greyson isn't the sleepy village it was thirty years ago. Change is scary for a lot of people." She pulled more of the strip off of the sticky part of the skirt and pressed the skirt into place, Jean feeding her the excess in short sections.

"You don't seem to mind change."

Karen shrugged. "I like new things. I never got to travel much so if I can't go to the change, let it come to me. Besides, new people bring fresh perspectives and opportunities. It's good for the town to get the dust knocked off of it once in awhile."

"Do you know that Arris is the prime suspect?"

There was a pause as Karen stood up and stared at

Jean. She took a deep breath. "I can see how that would be a first thought." She resumed sticking the skirt to the table. "No." She shook her head. "I don't think so. I've worked with Arris on the Fair Board for years. I've never seen the guy get mad or lose his cool."

Jean handed Karen the scissors to trim the excess skirting at the end of the table. "I never got a crazy vibe from him, that's true. But I've only known him a few months."

"You've only known me a few months." Karen made a crazy face. "How do you know I'm not crazy?"

Jean laughed. "Because we go to lunch together at least once a week, hiking at least once a month. You're a little strange but you aren't crazy."

"Why, thank you." Karen gave her head a few tics, then resumed sticking table skirt to the next table. "Did Nick say that Arris was a suspect?"

"Not in so many words. But he knows Arris controls the keys to that Conex." She fed Karen more skirt. "I don't like that he's a suspect. What if people don't come to the fair because of that kind of rumor?"

"Oh." Karen stopped sticking the skirt. "I hadn't thought of that. That would be awful. What can we do?"

Jean sighed. "I don't have a clue but it would be nice if we could do something."

"Hmm." Karen went back to the table skirt. "Yes, it would."

CHAPTER SIX

Nick White looked up from the reports on his desk at a rap on the door. Before he could say come in, the door opened. A balding, sandy-haired, six-foot-tall man with a small paunch came into the room. His blue eyes crinkled when he grinned. "Say thank you." Police Lieutenant Paul Oliver was Nick's best friend, and also the second-in-command of the Greyson Police station.

Nick put down his pen and leaned on his desk with both elbows. "For what?"

"For running interference between you and the Mayor."

Nick lounged back into his desk chair. "Don't tell me. Ed wants answers about the murder of Ida Grange?"

Paul dropped into one of the chairs in front of Nick's desk raised his ankle to his knee. "Yep, called to threaten to come over here or the morgue to demand answers. I told him it was too early for any answers, that we were still cataloging evidence."

"How'd that play?"

"About as well as you'd think," Paul chuckled. "He doesn't want Greyson to look like a bunch of hicks on the six o'clock news."

Nick sighed. Murders weren't common in Greyson. People were going to wonder if a small-town police chief could handle it. "I don't want Greyson to look bad on TV either, but like I told that fair volunteer, Jean Hays, at lunch time. I can't do miracles. The lab needs time. Ed Paige and Jean Hays are both going to have to wait."

"Isn't that the woman who found the body? She wants to know who did it already?"

Nick waved his hand in dismissal. "That's not it. She wants the bins from the container. Says they hold her ribbons. The judging is day after tomorrow and she wanted the bins processed first so she can have them back."

"Can't we do that? Seems a reasonable request. Those ribbons cost a lot of money and are ordered months in advance. Going to be a pretty bleak fair with no award ribbons hanging on the exhibits."

"She can wait her turn. Another easterner come out here to show the yokels how it's done. No, she can wait like everybody else."

Paul cocked an eyebrow. "She kick your dog or something? You sound ticked off."

Nick scowled. "Don't be a shit. Her attitude this morning when I interviewed her just pissed me off. Top of her head barely reaches my shoulder and she was making comments about how it couldn't be Arris, 'cause it would be stupid for him to hide a body in a container he held the keys to."

"Well, that's kind of true, Nick. It would be

stupid."

"I don't need her telling me how to do my job, that's all." Nick picked up his mug and sipped his coffee. "And she's a transplant, hasn't been here a year and she's already in charge at the fair."

"Ah, that's it then. She's an invader." Paul snorted. "The town's growing, Nick. It's a nice place, people are going to like it and move here. It's a good thing. We finally have stores and restaurants that stay open past five in the afternoon."

Nick shook his head. "It was nicer before, quieter."

Paul stood up. "I grant you that, but I like it now. We don't have to drive an hour and a half to Phoenix to go shopping. I can get pretty much everything I need right here in town. I like that."

Nick picked up his pen. "I guess that is an advantage." He waved Paul away. "Go question Arris Van Horn. I don't really think he did it but he's top of the list."

"Sure thing. I'll keep you posted." Paul walked to the door and opened it. "Oh, when are you going to release the victim's name?"

"The morgue is checking the dental records. The dentist is here in town. Once the ID is confirmed, I'll send a statement to the press."

Paul nodded. "And cut that woman some slack. Call the tech and have them process the bins first. If my wife doesn't get a ribbon on her pickles she's gonna be pissed."

Nick sighed. "Yeah. I guess. I'll call the lab. Go on now. You're a pain in my ass."

Paul laughed as he left the room.

CHAPTER SEVEN

By seven o'clock that night Jean was the last one in the building. From the far end of the building she did a final walk through, her footsteps echoing off of the cement floor. The fans had been turned off making it quiet in the building after the set-up racket all day. The separate areas looked so nice; Canning, Fine Arts, Photography, Floriculture, Agriculture and the others. They were all ready to accept submissions at noon tomorrow. She checked the other end door to make sure it was locked, then walked back to the middle door.

Arris had given her the key. A last look around and she flipped off the lights and stepped out into the night. The bugs flew around the light over the door as she locked it. A bat flew by her head and snapped one of the bugs out of the air, making her heart jump. She stepped away from the door and watched from twenty feet away. The light was a bug magnet and the bats were taking full advantage of it. One swooped in for the kill every minute or so. There were birds doing the same thing. Okay. Jean smiled. Restaurant is open, all-you-can-eat-food bar.

Her feet hurt. She'd been standing up most of the day. What she really wanted was to go home and get in her spa and relax with a glass of pinot grigio. Instead, she was going to have to go to the grocery and get food. Poor planning, she told herself as she walked to the car. *And you a project manager. Next year remember to stock the house so you don't have to go anywhere after a long day here.*

She got in her car and drove to the megamart, Ingram's. The traffic was light. *Maybe the locals think the town has gotten busy but the evening traffic doesn't prove it.* She turned into the store parking lot. A dual-purpose store—general goods, clothes, and electronics—it also had a grocery side. The original residents said it had come into town twenty years ago and was a blessing.

Jean mentally shrugged. It was just like every other Ingram's on the planet. However, based on comments concerning the stores in town before it came, it was very convenient. She turned into the deli area from the front door. Hmm, pizza or rotisserie chicken? Maybe a pre-made sub? She was standing in the middle of the space when a shopping cart glided past her.

"He's not worth it."

Jean blinked, jerked her mind out of the interior discussion of dinner choices and stared. A middle-aged woman, thin to emaciation, with hair dyed blond to the point of death and make-up that belonged in 1980s Alabama stood next to her.

"Excuse me?" Jean had a hard time making sense of the statement.

"Arris. He's a waste of time."

Still befuddled, Jean asked, "And who are you?"

"Analise. Arris's ex-wife. He's a player, always has been. And you're the new woman. On the fair board, all friendly with him." She shook her head. Jean noticed that the hair didn't move at all. "Don't bother."

"I'm not—"

"Oh yeah, that's what they all say." The woman looked her up and down. "I know who you are, Jean Hays. Divorcee, new in town, looking for a new husband, maybe. But they play. Oh yes. They play."

Jean felt a wave of heat flush over her. "But I never..." She groped for words. "I wouldn't..."

Analise waved her hand. "You don't have to tell me. But you're wasting your time. He never sticks around long. I learned that to my own regret. Stay away from him if you know what's good for you." She sashayed to the end of the deli counter, around the corner into produce, then frozen foods and the she was gone.

Jean watched her until she was out of sight. Her heart raced and her hands were sweaty on her purse and the cloth grocery bag she'd brought in with her. She felt a little like Alice going down the rabbit hole. *Did that just happen? What did I do to her? Arris has never made any sort of pass at me, not a hint. I know I didn't flirt with him.* Jean glanced quickly around the store; no one seemed to be looking at her. *Should I say something to Arris?* A deep breath calmed her down somewhat.

Still unnerved, she grabbed the nearest sub from the pre-made subs cooler and dropped it in her bag—lunch tomorrow. At the pizza cooler she grabbed a pre-made pizza—supper tonight. As she passed the rotisserie chicken, she picked one of those up, too.

Dinner tomorrow. She arrowed straight for the check-out line and tapped her foot with impatience as she waited her turn. The chicken next to her on the conveyer belt smelled wonderful. That was when the picture of the dead woman falling popped back into her mind. No more chicken for her. Jean's stomach rolled at the thought.

She had her credit card out and ready as soon as the teen-aged girl tapped the last register button. The girl pulled the register tape and handed it to her. "Thank you for shopping at Ingram's."

With an automatic, "You're welcome," Jean grabbed her bag and headed for the door.

At home she put everything in the fridge but the pizza. After reading the directions she set the oven to preheat and put her pizza stone inside. She went to the bathroom and started the water running in the garden tub. She poured an Epsom salt mixture into the tub that smelled of lavender. Her feet still hurt and that would help. After lighting a few candles, she went to the bedroom and got out of her hiking boots and sweaty clothes and put on her bathrobe.

In the kitchen she shoved the pizza in the oven and poured a glass of wine. By the time she got back to the bathroom, the tub was full. She could see the steam coming off of the water. The lavender she'd put in the home-made Epsom salt mix smelled wonderful. She could hardly wait. The timer went off in the kitchen. Pizza out, cut and on a tray, the glass of wine next to it she brought the rest of the bottle with her.

In the bathroom she pulled a chair next to the tub where she put the tray of food and wine. She brought her book from the bed table and, dropping the robe, climbed into the almost too hot water. "Ahh," escaped her lips as she slid in. The hot water and the lavender fragrance immediately relaxed her tightly strung muscles. "That's what I needed," she murmured. Eyes closed, she relaxed and let the water do its work.

Her mind wandered to the dead woman. Who was she? Did she die in that cabinet? Why was she killed? She wished she could do something about it. No one deserved to die like that. Abandoned, forgotten.

Don't be maudlin. Jean shook herself and pushed those sad thoughts out of her head. She grabbed her book, made sure the wine glass was within reach, and took a slice of pizza. She bit into it, cheese still melty, pepperoni salty and the dough a little charred on the edges. "Mmmm."

She didn't come out of the tub till the water was cold.

CHAPTER EIGHT

The next morning, Jean cut the foot-long sub in half. *Dang, it's vegetarian.* Her shoulders slumped. A combo would have been better. "That's what I get for just grabbing and not looking at them," she muttered. She slathered one half with mayo on one side and brown mustard on the other and wrapped the thing in plastic wrap.

Her thoughts returned to Analise and the accusations. *I don't know why she'd do that last night. Do other people think Arris and I are together?* The thought embarrassed her. But Analise was divorced from the man, so why so full of venom? Jean's next thought was of her own divorce. A lump rose in her throat just thinking about it.

That was three years ago. She still fumed at the memory. Dwight had left her with the car and the house but had drained the bank account. Her lawyer had gotten her a decent alimony and with her Air Force retirement she was doing all right financially, especially after she sold the house. But the insult he'd delivered still made her stomach churn. "Not exciting enough," she mumbled as she stabbed the knife into the peanut butter jar.

She slapped the peanut butter on her toast and bit the slice with a vengeance. Jean sipped her tea to wash the peanut butter down. After a deep breath she calmly screwed the lid on the peanut butter jar and put it back in the pantry. *I'm exciting. I'm just not twenty.* She snorted. *No matter, Jean. You've got a great life here. Forget that bastard.*

Jean finished her breakfast, washed up the few things from last night and this morning and headed out the door. She had a fair to put on.

It was ten thirty when Jean got to the Exhibits building. It was already hot inside. She was beginning to sweat as she opened all the doors, turned on the fans and the lights and readied herself for the day. Exhibitors would start arriving at noon. The Superintendents and their volunteers would be there at eleven or so to get ready. Having been a fair exhibitor herself, Jean understood how important it was to have all of the departments ready to accept the entries, tag them properly and ready them for tomorrow's judging.

Jean fretted about the ribbons. What if the police don't release the bins? She sipped her iced tea. She dragged the cooler outside, opened the valve and let the water drain out. Back inside she pulled a case of water bottles apart and dropped them in the cooler along with a fresh bag of ice. Just as she took another drink of tea, Karen came in through the middle doors.

"Ha, I thought you'd be here already."

"Just finished replenishing the cooler with water.

You're here early, too."

Karen dropped her things on a stand, then tucked them on a shelf hidden by the skirts she'd put up yesterday. "I have two volunteers working with me today that have never worked exhibit submissions. I want to go over everything with them before it gets started." She pulled three copies of fair books and a handful of pens out of her tote and put them on the folding table in front of her. "Any word on the ribbons?"

"No, I've been fretting and fuming about it all morning. Did anyone have any ideas?"

"Not a one. I asked everyone while you were out yesterday afternoon. They're a little more than worried."

"Me, too." Jean wiped the sweat from her temples as she thought about the problem. "I'll call Arris. He's been running the fair for years. Maybe he has some idea." She pulled her cell phone out of her shorts pocket and dialed his number. She was disappointed when it went to voicemail. "Hi, Arris. This is Jean. Can you call me or stop by Exhibits? The cops have our ribbons and I need some advice." She clicked off and sighed. "Hope he gets back to me soon."

It was twelve thirty and people were lined up in front of tables in every department with items they wanted to show at the fair. Some people had their children's little red wagons full of things, other people had just one or two items. Nervous before noon, Jean was beginning to relax. She could see Karen working her department, looking cool as a cucumber. Everything seemed to be going well. No one had a problem she needed to resolve. She popped open a bottle of water and sat down next to the middle door, out of the sun.

"Hey, Jean."

She looked out the door. Arris was walking up. He had on blue jeans, cowboy boots, a work shirt and a dirty cowboy hat.

"Hey, Arris. Come on in out of the sun." Jean pulled a chair over next to her. "Take a load off. Would you like some water?"

"Thanks, I think I will sit. And the water sounds good. I just helped my niece get her steer unloaded."

Jean handed him a new bottle of water. He twisted off the top and drank half the bottle. "Ah, that hits the spot." He put the cap back on the bottle and wiped his wet hands on his jeans. "I saw you called but I didn't listen to the message."

"Yeah, the cops kept our ribbon bins. I don't have anything for judging tomorrow."

He pulled a bandana out of his back pocket and wiped his face. "I was questioned yesterday as a person of interest."

"Oh no, Arris."

He nodded. "Yep, but I had nothing for them. Ina and I had a quarrel six months ago and she wouldn't return my calls. I figured she went travelling. She was always saying she wanted to travel around the world. I thought that's what happened."

"Oh no, Arris. But who is Ina?"

He reset his hat on his head. "That's right, you're new. Ina Grange. We dated for a few months. I've been dodging people all day. Half of them think I did it. The other half, well, I'm not sure if they believe me or are just nervous about the whole thing."

"I'm so sorry, Arris."

He tucked the bandana back into his pocket. "No

matter. I doubt the cops are going to release the bins in time. I'll call over to the Gila County Fair Board President. They may have ribbons we can use."

"Oh that would be great." Jean felt a whole load of worry disappear from her shoulders.

He scuffed his boots on the cement floor, eyes down. "I've got other news."

"What is it?" Her stomach clenched. This didn't sound good.

"I'm going to step down as Board President."

Jean panicked. *Leave the fair? All of his experience gone?*

"Just temporarily. Until all of this murder business is sorted out."

"But who will be in charge?"

He looked her in the eye. "You."

Jean could feel her stomach start to roll. "Me? I don't know how to run a fair. I'm new here. I don't know anything about it."

"The way the board is set up, VP of Exhibits is next in line. That's you."

She stared for a moment. "But, I don't have the contacts, the knowledge."

"I'll help. You can call me anytime."

She stared at him.

"I just don't think it's right for me to be such a public figure right now, since I'm a suspect in Ina's murder." He sat forward on the folding chair, elbows on knees. "People talk and, well, I think I just need to remove myself from the spotlight for a bit." He turned to look at her. "Temporarily, till I'm cleared."

She could see his point of view. It had to be very uncomfortable for people to suspect you. "Okay, I'll do my best. But you'll call about the ribbons?"

"Yeah." He stood up. "I'll call about the ribbons and let you know."

She stood up. "I don't think you killed anyone, Arris. Neither do the rest of the Superintendents."

He grimaced and nodded. "Thanks. That's appreciated." He turned to go out the door. "I'll get back to you."

"Oh, wait!"

Arris turned halfway out of the door.

Jean braced herself. "I met Analise last night at Ingram's. She seems to think we're having an affair."

He rolled his eyes. "She would. She thinks I'm having an affair with every woman over the age of eighteen in the whole county." Arris stepped back into the building. "I apologize. We've been divorced for years but she won't get past it." He took off his cowboy hat and ran his hand through his graying hair.

"So this isn't something everyone thinks is happening?" Jean swallowed hard.

"Oh gosh, no. It's just Analise. I'm sorry. Really. She has her own lovers but when she sees me out with someone she gets jealous."

"I'm sorry to bring it up. It's just..." She shrugged. "It was just embarrassing, accosted in the middle of the deli department and all." She could feel a blush creeping into her cheeks.

"I'll talk to her next time I see her, Jean. That is embarrassing. It won't do any good though." He sighed. "She'll just think it's true because I'm saying something about it."

"Don't do that, Arris. If it's not common gossip, I don't care what one person thinks. We know it's not so. Forget it." Jean certainly didn't want the woman's interest piqued.

"Are you sure?"

"I am," she nodded. "Forget I said anything. Call your friend then let me know where to go and who to talk to."

Arris put his hat back on. "Good. I'll do that." He left the building.

Jean dropped back into the folding chair, her fears about the possible rumors put to rest. She thought about her new position. "Great. Now I'm running the fair." She wiped the sweat off of her forehead with the back of her hand. It was going to be a long week.

CHAPTER NINE

They were in the middle of the afternoon slow-down. It seemed that most exhibitors either came early or after work. Most of the tables were near deserted, with just a handful of people scattered here and there. Karen came over to where Jean was sitting next to the cooler. "First rush is over."

"It seemed to go well. I had to referee a question in Canning but other than that, it's been pretty quiet."

"Shhh," Karen knocked on the wooden stand she was sitting beside. "You don't want to jinx yourself.

Jean told Karen that Arris had stepped down.

"Oh no! The poor man. You told him we don't believe he did it, didn't you?"

"I did. I felt so bad for him. He looked all beaten." Jean looked around the tent and lowered her voice. "Arris told me the victim's name, Ina Granger."

Karen's eyes bugged as she gasped. "Do you mean Grange?"

"Yeah. Did you know Ina Grange? Did Arris and Ina have a relationship?"

"Ina's the body?" Karen sighed. "That's why I didn't see her today."

"She enters stuff in your department?"

"Yep. She's a national-award-winning quilter. She's been written up in all the quilt magazines and is known internationally, too. Has gone on speaking tours and everything. Ina has entered something every year I've been the Superintendent and wins the Best of Show most of the time. It's such a shame. I suppose Vera is going to be thrilled this year." Jean was surprised by Karen's dry tone.

"Vera?"

Vera MacIlroy, Ina's biggest competitor. Last year when she came in and saw Ina had won Best of Show again she actually spit on the quilt. Everyone that was in the department just stood there slack-jawed as she vented on Ina. It was embarrassing."

"What did Ina do?"

"After Vera stormed off she took a tissue out of her pocket and wiped the spit off of the quilt, then went on with her conversation. It was a classy response."

"I'd say so. Wow. Competition runs stiff in the quilts, I guess."

"What a shame." Karen shook her head.

Jean nodded. She wanted to know more about Arris. "What about Arris and Ina?"

"Oh, yeah. Ina's family didn't approve at all. Arris has a reputation as a ladies' man. She was a widow with a grown son and they were afraid that Arris was after her money. That was silly. Arris came into money himself five years ago. Some relative or other left him a pile. Anyway, his ex-wife made all kinds of scenes whenever she ran into them in public." She sat down on the cooler lid. "Anyway, Analise and Arris have been divorced a good fifteen years. I don't know why she cared one way or the other."

"Maybe she was embarrassed or was concerned about how their kids felt."

"Doubt it. They never had kids. I think she was afraid Arris would spend his new money on the women. He didn't start dating Ina until a year ago or so. He actually took it kind of hard when she disappeared. Her family wouldn't talk to him at all."

"Oh, how sad. And now she's been found and it looks bad for Arris."

"It does." Karen nodded.

Jean watched her face. "You don't think he did it, do you?"

"Gosh no. He was attracted to the ladies but he had no reason to kill her." She looked thoughtfully at Jean for a moment. "Matter of fact, I don't think he's gone out on a date since she disappeared. He used to be a regular at the dances at Morgan's on Saturday nights. I've heard he hasn't been there in a long time."

"The place on Alpine and the highway? I haven't been to that restaurant yet."

"That's the one. Anyway, I heard Analise tried to get back with Arris after news got around about his inheritance." She waved her hand in disgust. "Total lack of character, if you ask me. He didn't buy it, of course. Maybe that's why she harassed him and his dates so much. Sad for him and embarrassing for her."

"What does she do for money?"

"She runs a food truck, fancy gourmet sandwiches. She's crazy but she can cook. They're delicious." Karen laughed. "She's one of the food vendors at the fair, you know."

Jean rolled her eyes. "Oh no. She isn't going to cause trouble is she?"

"No idea. But I heard from Barry—" She turned to Jean. "You know, Barry Cole, the Vendor Manager?"

"Oh, yeah," Jean nodded. "I haven't talked to him much but I remember him from the meetings."

"Yeah, well, *he* said she's a pain in the backside. Never happy with her location, the power, the number of people that stop at her truck, but she comes back every year."

"Sounds unpleasant."

"Yep."

"Glad I don't have to deal with her."

Karen nodded. "Thank your lucky stars."

"Arris is going to call Gila County about ribbons for me."

Karen smoothed the stray tendrils of hair back over her head. "That's awful. About him, I mean, not the ribbons. Hope they can spare some."

"Me, too."

John Gonzales walked up to them. "The gable fan at my end of the building has quit."

Karen stood up. "I'll let you get to it, then."

Jean stood also. "Let's take a look."

She and John walked to the east end of the building. The big fan up near the roof line was stock still. "I don't suppose we have a ladder that can get up there so we can see what's wrong?"

"No." He shook his head. "The tallest ladder in the Conex extends to fifteen feet." He eyed the fan. "That's gotta be twenty-five feet up."

Jean crossed her arms. "Well, if the only ladder is

in the Conex, the cops have it in any case. They took everything." A trickle of sweat started down her temple. "It's already getting hot in here." She looked at him. "I don't suppose *you* have a ladder that can reach?"

He scratched his head. "No, but call Arris. He'll get the right people." He stuck his hands in his pockets.

"I can't. He resigned. The cops have already been to question him and he thought it was too much of a controversy for him to be working the fair."

"He put you in charge?"

"Yep. Any ideas?"

He scratched his face. "Well, Edgar Conbeer does commercial electrical work. And now that I think about it, I think I've seen him here other years working on stuff."

"Thanks, John. I'll give him a call."

John turned to go.

"Oh, can you find some smaller fans? That may help."

"Yeah, no problem."

Forty minutes later Jean was standing with Edgar underneath the fan. "Oh yeah," he said as he viewed the area. "Let me go turn the electric off, then I'll come in and figure out what's wrong."

"Sure. Any estimate of how long this will take?"

"Not till I get up there. I'll let you know."

Jean nodded and walked over to John's department. Gems and Minerals was the nearest exhibit. "John, the electrician is going to shut off the power to the building. Can you give Edgar a hand if he needs it? I'll go tell everyone else it's going to be dim."

"Sure, Jean. Tough first day as the Board President." He wagged an eyebrow at her.

She laughed. "Kind of. Thanks for helping out."

He waved and she left to pass the word to the Superintendents. By the time she got back, Edgar had another guy with him and a ladder that reached all the way to the roof. Bags of tools lay on the floor.

"I'm hoping it's just a broken wire," he told her. "That can be resolved. If the motor is burned out, that fix will take longer."

"I'm crossing my fingers." She watched Edgar climb the ladder while his guy stood on the floor. She could see the electrician begin the examination at the power cord. She wondered if the fair was covered if he should fall.

People coming in to drop off exhibits stared. "Sorry it's dark in here," Jean told them. "A small electrical problem, it'll be fixed soon." They nodded and turned to their business. I hope, she thought. Please let it be something easy to fix. It was another fifteen minutes before Edgar called down. He was grinning.

"It's a crimped wire."

She breathed a shallow sigh of relief.

"I'll splice a new piece of wire in and we'll have the power on in just a few."

He was as good as his word and ten minutes later. Edgar handed her the bill. "After the fair you'll have to get a real repair but it should hold for the weekend."

"Thank you, Edgar. I appreciate it."

He nodded. "Rumor is all over town that the police suspect Arris. I don't believe a word of it. He's not that kind of man."

"I'll tell him you said that, Edgar. He's feeling a little friendless right now."

"Yeah, some people will believe anything. You tell him I said hi. Come on by the shop anytime."

Jean smiled at him. "I'll do that. Thank you again."

He nodded and left. *That was easy enough.* She tucked the bill into her binder. *Let's hope that's the last big problem this week.* But she didn't think she'd get off that easy.

CHAPTER TEN

Nick White was at his desk when Greta Kaufman, his secretary, buzzed his phone. He hit the intercom button. "Yeah."

"Chief, the Mayor's on line two."

Nick closed his eyes and took a deep breath. He knew what this call was about. The mayor expected cop-show speed to solve this murder. The man watched too much TV. "I've got it," he said as he eyed the blinking light on the phone. He clicked off the intercom and paused before he punched the button for line two. "Mayor."

"Nick."

The Mayor sounded as though he were practicing for the local theater group. Nick knew better. Mayor Ed Paige was a good man; he was friends with a lot of the people in Greyson, that's why he kept getting elected. But the man didn't have a logical bone in his body. The council kept him on track. "What can I do for you, Ed?"

Nick heard the man sputter on the other end of

the line. "I need some answers about Ina's death, Nick. I thought that would be obvious. Her family is calling the office, calling my house. I need to tell them something."

Nick could feel the heat rise just as the air conditioning fan kicked on in his office. He took a breath. He had known it would be like this when they went to do the family notification and told the press. "It's not TV, Ed. It takes time to examine the body and the evidence."

"So you're doing nothing?" The Mayor's voice squeaked.

Nick's hand gripped the handset harder. "We're talking to persons of interest, we're examining evidence, we're talking to Ina's family to try and identify her timeline."

The Mayor took a deep breath. "I can sympathize with the process, Nick. But people want to know that something is being done."

"I appreciate your concern, Mayor. But I can't go any faster than the technicians can process evidence." *Can you give me a break, Ed?* He was probably calling from his dry cleaning business, Nick thought as he checked the wall clock. He probably had people coming in all day talking about the murder and he was getting nervous.

"I'm glad you can see my point of view, Nick. You'll call me as soon as you know something?"

Nick closed his eyes again. He'd never said he saw the man's point of view. "As soon as I can, Ed. As soon as I can."

Nick hung up and looked at the report in front of him. The coroner had put in a call to Phoenix for help. He just wasn't qualified to examine a body in such a state. It would be a day or more before anyone could come and help him. The evidence was being sorted slowly. Everything in the container had to be removed, tagged, logged, and the first thing to be fingerprinted was the double-door cabinet the body had fallen from. He snapped a finger against the report. Of course it had Arris's fingerprints on it. It also had fingerprints from pretty much everyone else in the county. *Not Ms. Hays's prints though. I guess she's too new. She's spunky, that's for sure. Must be that military background.*

He'd had her background run right after she came to his office. Twenty years in the Air Force, a project planner. Figures she'd pick up volunteer work like the fair. *Gutsy, coming in here like that.* He had considered Paul's suggestion that he help her out. He wanted to; his aunt had her prize roses entered in the fair. He shook his head. He just couldn't do it. First things had to be examined first, though the tubs had been close to the cabinet. They were up to be examined next.

Nick slapped the folder shut and tossed it in the Out box. Greta would retrieve it and bring it back full of information that told him nothing. He drummed his fingers on the desk. Arris could only tell the police that he and Ina had quarreled and he'd thought she took a trip. Time to check out Arris some more. His timeline was the next priority after Ina's.

He picked up the phone and punched some numbers into the dial. "Paul, get a guy on Arris's timeline. The last eight months. If he isn't the killer, maybe someone he or Ina knew well is."

"Sure, Nick. You want me to expand the search?"

"Yeah, let's expand the search. What if Arris is being set up? He might be one of the victims here."

The line was quiet for a moment. "Treading a fine line there, buddy. Some people might think you're protecting the guy."

Nick's boot tapped the floor under his desk. "Let them think. I'm not gonna railroad the man just because the Mayor wants an instant killer."

"Fair enough. I'll get on it."

Nick hung up. He was going to get flak for this, but he didn't care.

CHAPTER ELEVEN

At five pm, exhibit entries were still slow. "It's just the calm before the storm," Karen told Jean. Jean had stopped by Karen's department to see how it was going. "I let my volunteers go for half an hour to catch a break. How are you doing? Any more electrical problems?"

"No," Jean laughed. "One a day is sufficient. No problems over here?"

"Not a one." She looked up and down the building and in a low voice said, "I have an idea."

Jean's interest was piqued. "About?"

"Don't be a goose, Jean. About Ina's murder." The two women met at the end of Karen's processing table. "Look, I have a cousin, second cousin actually, who lives over in Rancho Verde. He knows one of Ina's lovers from before Arris."

Jean nodded. "And?"

"I say that after we get done here, we trot on over to my cousin's house and see what he knows."

Jean didn't feel good about this plan. "And then

what? We question him and he says so and so was Ina's lover, then we just go knock on the guy's door?"

"Yeah!" Karen was beaming. "Isn't this a great idea?"

Jean's eyebrow arched. "Well, no, not exactly. I mean, what if your cousin doesn't really know anything and we knock on some crazy guy's door? We could get killed."

Karen's eyes rolled. "No one is going to hurt us. This isn't Washington, D.C."

"I don't know, Karen." Jean thought about some of the places she'd been on projects for the Air Force. Places where you could get mugged for your sack lunch. "It sounds risky."

"Nonsense. My cousin will tell us if it's all right to visit whoever it is. Come on. Let's investigate."

Jean studied Karen's excited face. She sighed. This sounded like something for the police to look into but after hearing so much about Ina and Arris over the afternoon, her interest was piqued. "I guess. Meet me at the middle door when everyone is done. I have to shut stuff off and lock up."

Karen whooped. "Yes! This is going to be so much fun."

Jean snorted at Karen's enthusiasm. "Sure. A barrel of laughs."

CHAPTER TWELVE

While the rest of the Exhibits building was busy with people dropping off their entries, she pulled the card for Chief White's office out of her pocket. She dialed the number on her cell phone. Greta picked up. "Hi Greta, this is Jean Hays, we spoke yesterday?"

"Yes, Ms. Hays. I remember. What can I do for you?"

"Please, call me Jean. We're taking in a lot of exhibits. Is there any way to get my ribbon bins for tomorrow?" She crossed her fingers.

"I'm sorry, Jean, but everything is still in the lab. Should I get Chief White for you?"

He shoulders slumped. Memories of her last conversation with him flew through her mind. "No, no, thanks anyway. No need to bother the Chief. Look, if you can, would you call me as soon as the bins are released?"

Greta laughed. "Yes, I'll do what I can. My husband has a woodworking project he's entering as soon as he gets out of work. He'd hate not to have a ribbon."

"Thank you, Greta. I appreciate it."

"Good luck, Jean." She clicked off.

Jean turned her phone over and over in her hand. After a few moments she dialed Arris.

"Hello?"

"Arris, it's Jean. Sorry to bother you."

"Not a bother, Jean. What's the problem?"

Jean watched several people come into the building through the middle door and from both end doors. Lines were forming at the tables in every department. She put a hand over one ear to hear the call over the cacophony of voices. "It doesn't look as though the bins will be released. Did you call Gila County?"

"Yeah, sorry, I just got off the phone with my friend over there. They can supply the ribbons for the Exhibits building. I know that Jason Lerner, the VP of Livestock, has everything he needs for the livestock and horse competitions."

A wave of relief washed over Jean. "That's great, Arris. Can you go get them?"

"No, sorry, Jean. I'm sort of restricted to town at the moment."

"Oh," she stammered, her face suddenly flushed. "Of course."

"I'll give you my friend's name and number and you can call him to meet and get the ribbons."

"Wonderful. Wait, let me get a pen and paper."

She took down the information and sighed. "I'm so sorry about this, Arris. What a disaster."

"No worries. I know I didn't do it. I'm going to help Nick with whatever I can."

Jean was surprised. "You know Chief White?"

"Of course, I was his 4-H leader back in the day. The boy raised some mighty fine beef. He's a good man. He'll be fair."

I should have figured. "I'm glad you have confidence in him, Arris. He treated me like rotten cheese."

Arris laughed. "Yeah, he's a hometown boy. Came home as soon as he finished college. He did well, summa cum laude in Criminal Justice."

Her mouth fell open. "I didn't know. I'll remember that, Arris. Take it easy, okay?"

"Sure. Remember to call me if there's a problem. I heard you handled the electrical problem just fine."

"You heard about that?"

He laughed again. "Small town, Jean. Small town." He hung up.

Jean clicked off. *I have to remember everyone knows everything in a small town.* She checked the number she wrote and dialed. Time to set up getting those ribbons.

CHAPTER THIRTEEN

Nick stood on the stoop outside Arris Van Horn's house. The place hadn't changed much from when he was a boy coming here for 4-H meetings. The porch had been expanded to cover the entire front of the log cabin instead of just a small roof over the door. The landscaping had matured. Arris's first wife had planted roses which he kept up despite Analise's attempts to have them removed. They were well shaped and had been deadheaded recently. Arris's pick-up truck was parked in front of the separate garage, also log-built. He remembered the huge stack of ponderosa pine Arris had piled near the spot where the garage now stood. The man had built it himself with a little help from friends and using the wood from his own property.

Nick had always admired that kind of self-sufficiency. Forest green shutters were hooked open and freshly painted. Arris wasn't the kind of man to let things slide. That was the main reason Nick didn't think he had anything to do with Ina's death.

The door opened. "Nick! Good to see you, son." Arris held out his hand.

Nick shook it. "Sorry to intrude, Arris, but I have to ask you some questions."

"Not a problem, Nick. Come on in. Coffee?"

Nick stepped in and closed the door behind him. "Yeah, that would be good." He looked around. Even though Arris didn't have a wife, everything was clean and orderly. The curtains were neat and open. The coffee table was dust free, magazines stacked neatly at one end except for one that was lying open. He followed Arris to the kitchen.

It was just as he had remembered it. A big table that could seat ten people sat in front of a bay window looking out to the back yard and the barn. A stove was mounted in the island where a coffee pot was plugged in and half full.

Arris pulled a couple of mugs out of the cupboard. "Milk? Sugar?"

"Yeah. Thanks."

Arris opened the fridge and retrieved a carton of half and half. Then he opened the cupboard opposite the range and picked up a ceramic sugar bowl, which he put on the island next to the coffee pot. "Sorry you had to drive way out here." Arris lived north of town, half-way up the Moggollon rim in a small community of ranchers.

"It's just a few minutes' drive, Arris."

"I thought your friend Paul had already asked all the questions you had." He poured coffee into each mug then pushed one toward Nick. He got a spoon out of a drawer next to the sink and handed it to Nick.

"He did. I have some more." Nick put a spoon of

sugar in his mug, then a splash of half and half. He stirred. "Tell me about you and Ina."

Arris picked up his mug and sat down at the table. He sipped his coffee as he looked out the window at a pair of horses grazing in the field next to the barn. "Not much to tell. We got along well, went dancing. Had some fun."

Nick followed him over and sat at the end of the table so he could see Arris's face. "That's it? You just had fun? What was the argument about?"

After another sip he said, "I don't want to tell tales, Nick. It's over. What does it matter now?"

Nick saw the sadness on his mentor's face. "I have to ask, Arris. It's the only way I can clear your name. What was the argument about?"

Arris ran his hand over his brush-cut gray hair. "Have you talked to Ina's family?"

"We are." He sipped his coffee. It was a little cold. "But let me get the info from you."

"She gambled. You might know that already."

Nick nodded encouragement. He hadn't known that.

"The Apaches put that casino in twenty years ago. Ina loved it. It wasn't a big deal at first. I'd seen her there myself, back in the day. But it wasn't until I started stepping out with her that I realized she had a problem."

"I understand." Nick *did* understand. The casino was great for the tribe but it was hell on wheels for some of the people in the community that couldn't seem to leave it alone. A good bit of the crime in town came from people robbing convenience stores and ripping off open cars for cash to pay gambling debts. "So what happened?

"I mentioned it a few times, how I noticed she had no food in the house or when she borrowed money from me to pay the light bill." He shook his head. "I sat down with her just before she disappeared and tried to get her to get some help." He stared out at the horses again. "She had a melt-down. She threw a candy dish at me, screamed and cried. I felt terrible."

"Where did this happen, Arris?"

"Her house. I was there to pick her up to go dancing. A couple of the tribe were just leaving. When she answered the door she was in tears. I asked her what the tribe people were doing at her door. That's when it all came apart." He drank again. "I left after she threw me out. Called me judgmental, as bad as her family." Arris turned to Nick. "I wasn't judging her, Nick. But she had a gambling problem. I was trying to help."

Nick saw the man's eyes go red with unshed tears. "I'm sorry, Arris. She wasn't the only one in town with a problem." He saw Arris shrug. "And you didn't see her again?"

"No." Arris shook his head. "I tried to call her for a few days but I kept getting her machine. Then I got a message that the machine was full and couldn't take any more messages. I didn't know what else to do. I stopped by a few times and knocked on the door. I asked around but no one had seen her. I figured she'd just decided to take one of those long cruises she always talked about."

"I'm sorry, Arris."

"I should have done more."

"I'll talk to her family, see what they can tell me about any problems she had with the gambling. I'll check the phone records, too. You know, to verify your story."

Arris just nodded.

Nick stood up. "I don't think you did this horrible thing, Arris. But I have to check."

Arris slid his chair back and stood. He walked Nick to the door. "I know you do, son." When Nick stepped out onto the porch he said, "Just find out who did this, would you?"

"I will, Arris." Nick walked back to his SUV. He definitely wanted to talk to her family. Then the casino. Was the casino strong-arming delinquent debtors? He'd have to look into that.

CHAPTER FOURTEEN

It was after seven pm when Jean locked the door to the Exhibits building. "That was quite a rush of people at the end," she told Karen.

"Happens every year. We say we close at six, and then fifty people rush in at five fifty-nine. I don't usually mind; they're getting off work and stuff. But today we want to get out and we get more at the last minute than usual."

The two women walked to the cars. Jean was grateful for the fresh air. As soon as the sun went down it began cooling off. It was a pleasant eighty degrees right now. She could hear the livestock in the livestock barns and kids playing music. A lot of laughter floated through the air. "They're having fun."

"Yep. They're here till Sunday night, when they load their market animals onto the slaughter truck. Then there'll be tears. Poor things. But right now they're excited and ready to show their animals."

Jean nodded to the security guard. Now that there were valuables in the Exhibit Building, they'd hired someone to keep an eye on things. He locked the gate behind them. Once in the car, Jean asked, "Want to get something to eat? We can hit a drive-thru and eat on the way."

"Great idea."

Fifteen minutes later Jean was driving east on Highway 620, heading for Rancho Verde. They ate quietly. Karen gathered up the paper trash and stuffed it in one of the takeout bags. "Just toss it behind my seat, I'll clean it out later," Jean instructed Karen as she wiped her hands on the last napkin. "What's your cousin's name?"

Karen settled back into her seat. "Ari Robertson. His mother is of Greek descent and she named him for some uncle of hers."

"And how did you know to call him about Ina?" Jean adjusted her rear view-mirror to cut the glare from following cars.

"I called around. Friends, cousins, neighbors, anyone I could think of. Ari said he may know something and I told him I'd bring you down."

"Ah. I just wondered."

The two women spent the rest of the trip talking about the day's events on the fairgrounds. It took them half an hour to get to Rancho Verde. Karen directed Jean to her cousin's house.

They parked in the driveway and got out of the car. "Geesh, must be ninety down here."

"Yeah, they're three thousand feet lower than Greyson. It's more desert here. That's why the river was such a big deal to early ranchers."

Jean looked at the house. It was a manufactured home set on a barren spot of land. There were no trees around the house for shade, though a few cactuses were scattered around the yard. Lights showed through the living-room and kitchen windows. "Let's get this done." Jean felt a little ridiculous for doing this. She wasn't a cop but it just bugged her that Arris was being railroaded. She followed her friend to the door. Karen rang the doorbell.

It was opened by a man holding a two-year-old child, a girl by the look of her pajamas. "Hey, Karen. Glad to see you." The girl stared at them with big brown eyes and her thumb and forefinger stuck in her mouth. "Come on in."

Once inside, Karen made introductions. "Ari, this is my friend Jean. Jean, my cousin Ari and," she grinned at the baby, "my newest cousin, Lea." She cooed at the baby.

"Nice to meet you, Ari, Lea." Jean smiled at the girl. She didn't hold out her arms or try to touch her. It had bugged her no end when her boy, Jim, was poked and grabbed as a baby.

"Want coffee or something?" He shifted the child to the other arm.

"No, we just ate. Thank you though," Jean told him.

"Come on into the kitchen."

As they followed him she noticed that the floor was covered with toys, but otherwise it was a nice little house. Art hung on the walls, photographs of family seemed to cover every horizontal surface. "Sorry about the mess," Ari said as he sat down at the island counter. "My wife has a craft project all over the table. Are you sure I can't get you something?"

Karen shook her head. "Really, we're good."

Jean sat at the end, next to Karen. "I appreciate

you seeing us, Ari. What can you tell us?"

"I have an acquaintance, Josh Marlow, that I know went with Ina before she started seeing Arris. We were friends as kids but, not to speak bad of the guy, he's not much of a success as an adult. He was in the military for awhile but came back after his first tour. He works over at the K Bar Seven at the south end of Rancho Verde as a cowhand. He lives in the doublewide they keep for the hands."

Jean was surprised. She had no idea there were still cowhands. "He's divorced?"

Ari smoothed his daughter's brown curls. "No, he never married. He thinks he's a player, but really any woman he's gone out with has pegged him for what he is and moved on."

"Why do you think he's suspicious?"

He answered after blowing his daughter a kiss. "He was angry at Ina for dumping him. He made it pretty clear at the local bar that she had made a big mistake."

"You think he's capable of murder?" Jean asked him.

"I'd like to say no, but he came back from Afghanistan different." He looked at both women, his head shaking. "I don't know. I hope not."

Jean got up. "Thank you for meeting with us. I appreciate it."

"Me too," Karen said as she rose. "Let me give that darling a smooch." Ari handed over the baby, whose face began to screw up, eyes big with fear. "Don't worry, sweetie. Cousin Karen won't hurt you." She gave the girl a kiss on the cheek and handed her back to her father before she decided to cry.

He walked them to the door. "We've got to get together more often, Karen. Come down after the fair. I'll call some of the rest of the family and we'll have a barbeque."

"Sounds good, Ari."

The women walked to the car. Karen waved before she got in. In just a moment, they were back out on the highway. Jean was nervous about meeting this cowhand. He sounded like a jerk and really, her ex was the last jerk she'd hoped to have to deal with.

CHAPTER FIFTEEN

Karen directed Jean to the K Bar Seven ranch. "How do we find the double-wide?" Jean asked.

"There may be a sign but it's probably near the barns. We'll drive in and see. If we have to, we'll stop at the house and ask."

"People are okay with random cars driving around their property?"

"We're not random. We're visiting."

Jean laughed. "That'll be good to remember when we have a shotgun pointed at us."

It turned out to be easier than Jean expected. There was a sign to the bunkhouse, as well as to the main house, the barns, several corrals and the grain barn. Jean parked outside the bunkhouse. Every light in the place was on, shining out to the parking lot. There were four pickups parked in front of the front door. "This must be the place."

Karen got out and Jean followed. She walked right up the three wooden steps to the front door and knocked. There was no porch or even a small deck. A young man, mid-twenties, dressed in a soft cotton plaid work shirt, jeans and with bare feet answered the door. "Yeah?"

"We're looking for Josh Marlow," Karen told him.

He stepped inside, leaving the door ajar. "Josh, two ladies here to see you."

The women could hear the TV blasting and some guys laughing and hooting. One voice called out, "Way to go, dude!"

Another shouted, "Hey, you need to share."

More laughing, then someone said, "Shut up."

The door flew open. A middle-aged man stood there, black hair going gray curled over his ears. He had on a faded denim work shirt, jeans and flip-flops. He looked them over, then scratched at the three-day-old-beard, also going gray. "Do I know you?"

Karen backed down the steps. "No, we've never met, but my cousin Ari Robertson told me where you were."

Josh looked them over, then came outside, closing the door behind him. As he came down the steps, Jean noticed he was slender but well muscled. She and Karen stood together. He stopped about three feet from them. "What's this about?" There was just enough light from the windows to see his brown eyes studying them.

"Did you hear that Ina Grange died?" Jean asked.

"I heard." He stuck his hands in his back pockets. "What of it, and who are you?"

Jean didn't have a good feeling about this, out here in the dark on a strange ranch with a guy she suspected of killing someone. "Well, I found the body and it's been bothering me, you know, her death. So I thought I'd find some of her friends and, uh, talk to them. I'm Jean Hays and this is Ari's cousin, Karen."

He turned his head and spit out into the dark. "So?"

Jean gathered up her courage in the face of his defiance. "Did you know her well?"

Josh smirked. "We partied. I had to dump her though, after awhile." He stared at Jean. "Your name sounds familiar. You from around here?"

"No, I just moved here a few months ago." Jean fidgeted with the seam of her shorts. Her hands had grown sweaty. "I heard Ina dumped you for Arris Van Horn."

He scowled and jerked his hand out of his pocket. He pointed his finger at them. "That's a damn lie. No skanky cow ever dumped me. I dumped her."

Despite the jolt of fear that bolted through her, Jean asked, "I heard she had money and that's why you dated her."

His mouth opened, then shut. "I'm no toy boy," he said through clenched teeth. "She had a problem."

"What problem?"

"She couldn't stay out of the casino. She blew through money faster than anyone I've ever seen." He peered at Jean again. "I know your name from somewhere. You have a relative named Dwight?"

Jean's breath stopped in her throat as a wave of surprise washed over her. "My ex-husband's name is Dwight."

"Dwight Hays." Josh slapped a hand on his thigh. "I knew it! Me and him went to tech school together. I washed out and spent the rest of my time in the Air Force in Afghanistan drivin' trucks. The military sucked. Afghanistan sucked. I came home."

His face clouded and he pointed a finger at them

again. "Don't be tryin' to pin Ina's murder on me. I ain't seen her since last November."

"You weren't mad when she started dating Arris?"

"No, I got enough problems of my own. I don't need any of somebody else's." He turned back to the house, then spun around. "I ain't seen her since November," he scowled at them. "Best you remember that." He turned again and pounded up the steps and into the house, slamming the door behind him.

The sound of the other men questioning him drifted out to them over the sound of the TV. "I'm not sure that was helpful," Jean said as they walked to the car.

"He seemed pretty defensive about the last time he saw Ina," Karen offered as she got in and shut the door.

"Yeah. He did. Did you know Ina had a gambling problem?" Jean started the car and turned it around.

"No, I didn't. That's a shame. She was a nice person, really." When they'd covered the long driveway and were back on the highway, Karen asked, "What about him knowing your ex?"

"Two peas in a pod, I'd say. They must have been best buds in tech school."

"Small world."

"Yeah, small world." Jean gripped the steering wheel. Talking to Josh was like talking to Dwight. Everything snarky and slimy. She swallowed her distaste of both men and focused on Ina. First, it's Analise and jealousy over Arris, then Vera and stiff quilting competition and now, a gambling problem. Would a sanctioned casino send bullies after a person? Would an aging woman kill over quilts? Jean had no idea.

CHAPTER SIXTEEN

It was nine thirty before Karen walked through the garage door into her kitchen. Home-sewn curtains hung at the windows, white with embroidered cactuses on them. They were pulled so the neighbors, just thirty feet away, couldn't see in. The kitchen had hand-painted ceramic tiles for a backsplash and similar tiles covered the wall behind the stove. Pale yellow paint covered the exposed walls. Karen loved how the room glowed when the sun shone through the windows. She loved her house but sometimes she wished she didn't live in a development with only a fifth of an acre for the house and yard. She dropped her purse and keys on the counter next to the door.

She found her twenty-two-year-old daughter, Peggy, in the kitchen, setting up the coffee pot for the next morning. "Hi, Mom. You're home late. Everything all right at the fair?"

"Yeah." Karen went to the fridge and removed a pitcher of iced tea. She poured a glass, put the pitcher back and sat down at the table. "The fan failed, making the building hot as hell. Jean handled it well. There were a lot more entries this year than last. I'm glad. I like to see a lot of people involved."

Peggy sat at the table with her mother. She smoothed the crocheted place mat in front of her. It had the cactus theme as well. "So you had to stay three extra hours?"

"No." Karen waved her hand. "We went to talk to your cousin Ari, who gave us a lead on a guy named Josh Marlow who was one of Ina's lovers just before Arris. We thought he might know something about her death." She drank a quarter of the glass of tea. "Gosh, I'm so thirsty tonight."

"Mom, you and Jean went to talk to this guy? Thinking he might be a killer?" Peggy's voice rose to a squeak.

"He was a bit peeved but he was all right." She yawned and rubbed her eyes. It had been a long day in the heat. She wanted nothing better than to get a shower and go to bed.

"Jeez, Mom. You could have been killed!"

"I don't think so. The guy is a jerk but I don't know if he'd be capable of killing anyone." She decided to refrain from telling her daughter the guy spent time in the Air Force in Afghanistan. "How about you? How was the doctor's office today?" Her daughter worked as a receptionist in the office of a local general practitioner.

"I kept the files in order, but it was a struggle. The doctor just takes things willy-nilly. No wonder they're such a mess. I went to class at six; I barely had time to get out of the office and over to the college. It was a lab today, our first practice giving shots. They use oranges." She made a face. "The instructor says that's exactly what it feels like when you give a person a shot."

Karen shuddered. She never was attracted to the medical field—too many fluids for her taste. Having a baby had been bad enough. "Did you get the hang of it?"

"It was weird at first, but I think I have it down. Tyler met me afterward and took me to the diner for supper."

Karen nodded but inwardly wished her daughter would date someone else. Tyler was twenty-five and still trying to find himself. She thought he was going to end up like Josh Marlow: working hard labor, seasonal jobs and on welfare the rest of the time. "That's nice." She finished her tea. "We still don't have ribbons. Jean will have to drive over to Gila County and borrow some from them tomorrow."

"Oh, Mom. How awful. Have you heard anything else about Ms. Grange? All the paper said was that it was being investigated."

"No." Karen stood up and walked to the sink to rinse her glass out. "Jean said everything from the container is being processed by the police." She wiped her hand on a tea towel she'd crocheted a top to. "I heard poor Arris has been questioned already."

Peggy rose from her chair. "How awful."

"I'm heading up to my room to take a shower and go to bed, honey. Are you staying up?"

"No, I'm going to my room to read my homework."

The two left the kitchen, turned out the lights and went upstairs.

#

Peggy slid out her desk chair and sat down after she pulled her cell phone out of her pocket. Her room still reflected her taste from her high school years. The space was decorated in pink and white with stuffed animals filling every flat spot in the room. Posters of teen heartthrobs were pinned to the walls. She hit the speed dial.

"Hi, Beautiful," she heard when it picked up.

"Hi, Tyler. Mom's finally home. I thought I'd call and say good-night." Peggy propped her elbows on the desk, shoving her textbook to the side.

"She say anything?"

"She said the cops still have their ribbons. They have to make a run to the next county to borrow some." She pulled her dark brown hair out of the ponytail it was in and rubbed the sore spot at the back of her head where it had been gathered. "She and Jean went to question some guy about his relationship with Ina Grange. I told her that was stupid. He could have killed them."

"Yeah, not a good move. What's his name?"

Peggy flopped back in her chair. "Uh, J something. Jason. No, not Jason. Josh, that was it."

"Oh, I don't recognize the name."

"Me neither, but how horrible for poor Mr. Van Horn. He's always been really nice to me."

There was a long pause before Tyler said, "Yeah. Nice guy."

Peggy yawned while she wondered about his tone. "Do you know him?"

"I've done some work for him. Kind of a hard-ass."

"Oh, I'm sorry, Tyler." She yawned again. "Look,

I've got a chapter to read before I go to bed. See you tomorrow?"

"Sure," Tyler promised. "When do you get off?"

She told him, then made kissy noises into the phone. "Night, Tyler."

"Night, Peg."

It occurred to her only after she clicked off to ask what he did for Arris. She'd try and remember to ask him tomorrow.

CHAPTER SEVENTEEN

Jean rose at six in the morning. She wanted to get over to her contact from the Gila County fair and get the ribbons, then get back so they could be put on the appropriate exhibits before too late in the day. After her usual cup of Earl Grey tea while she checked her email, she had two eggs scrambled with Swiss Chard and cherry tomatoes for breakfast. The tomatoes were a gift from Karen's garden. Jean hadn't felt confident enough about the climate to start a garden yet. Maybe next year. She washed up the dishes, then went back to her bedroom to change out of her t-shirt and knit shorts into a blouse and khaki shorts for the day.

She skipped taking a lunch, deciding to grab lunch at the fair or in town, depending on how long it took her to get back from Gila County. All that was left was to grab her keys and head out the door. She left the house through the door to the carport and locked it. It wasn't until she was right next to the car that she saw the words *STOP INVESTIGATING*, scrawled in soap across her windshield. She stopped short and stared, her mouth gone dry.

What? Who did this? She pulled her cell phone out of her pocket with shaky hands. Her eyes drifted over the rest of the car. That's when she noticed that the front driver's-side tire was flat. *Oh no!* A quick investigation showed that all four tires were flat. She looked around the carport. Nothing else seemed to be disturbed.

She dialed 911. "My car's been vandalized," she told the operator. She was redirected to the Police Department since the crime wasn't in progress. She spoke to Martha Horner. After a greeting, she gave the receptionist her address. "Yes, I'll be here." She clicked off, still shaking. Jean went to her door, unlocked it and went inside and sat down at the kitchen table. Her thoughts flew around and around in her brain in a panic. *Oh my God,* was all she could think. Ten minutes later there was a knock on the door. Jean jumped, then realized it must be the police. She opened the door, where a young male police officer stood.

"Ms. Hays?"

"Yes, yes, that's me."

They walked around the car together, the officer taking notes the whole while. Jean saw a tow truck pull up to the end of her driveway and stop next to the police cruiser. The officer noticed her attention had moved. His gaze followed hers out to the street. "Oh, yeah, we'll tow your car to the lab and have it dusted for fingerprints."

She nodded. Everything felt so surreal, as though she were underwater. The sunny day felt suddenly dark. "Um, yeah. Sure."

"Do you know anyone who would do this to your

property, Ms. Hays?"

She was watching the tow truck operator back into her driveway. "What?"

"Who would do this to you, Ms. Hays?"

Her mouth opened and closed twice before she could form any coherent thought. "No one. I mean, I don't know. I've only lived here a few months."

"What are you investigating, Ms. Hays?"

"Uhm." She watched the truck operator lower two ramps from the back of his truck. "I found the body."

"You're referring to the murder victim, Ina Grange?"

"Yes. I don't think Arris did it. I was asking around."

The young man frowned at her. "You shouldn't be interfering in police business, ma'am."

"No, yes." Flustered, she pulled her attention away from the truck and back to the officer. "I mean, you're right. I don't want to do that."

He nodded and slid the notebook into his pocket along with his pen. "Is there someone you can call? It's a shock to be vandalized like this."

She licked her lips. Call someone? "Yes, I can call my son."

The officer pulled the microphone from his shoulder and identified himself with a number. "Tow truck on scene. No injuries to the owner. Car had tires slashed and a warning soaped on the windshield."

"Understand, 103," came the static-laden reply. "Canvas the scene for any neighbors who might have seen something. Notify us when you've cleared the scene."

"Roger, base." He put the microphone back on his

shoulder. "Do you want someone to stay with you, Ms. Hays?"

She shook her head slowly back and forth. "No, I'll be fine. I'll call my son. Thank you, Officer."

She watched as the driver of the truck hooked chains to her car and pulled it up onto the flatbed. It took no time at all after that for him to retract his ramps and drive off with her car. The officer left and she was alone. Jean went into the house and sat down on the sofa. The digital clock on the DVR told her it was 09:34. So much for getting an early start. She called Karen. "Can you come and get me? My car tires were slashed. I don't have any way around."

"Oh my God! Are you all right?"

"Yeah, I'm fine. But I need to rent a car and I need to open the Exhibits building."

"I'll be right over, sweetie."

They clicked off. Jean sat staring out of her living room window to the street. Who would do this? Stop investigating. *I've only really talked to one person, Josh Marlow. Was it him? He found out where I live and he tracked me down? That can't be it. But who else could it be?*

Questions whirled around in her mind until the doorbell rang. Getting off of the sofa seemed to Jean to be very hard to do. Karen stood there when she opened the front door. She gave Jean a bear hug. "You're okay? You weren't hurt?"

"No." Jean put on a smile. "I'm fine, really. I just need to get a rental and get those ribbons."

Karen hugged her again. "That's the pioneer spirit. Come on, I'll get you over there and get you a car."

"No, fairgrounds first, so people can get in."

Karen patted her on the shoulder. "Yes, of course. I'll drive."

Jean nodded and they left. She locked the door behind her and tucked the keys in her pocket. It was going to be another long day.

CHAPTER EIGHTEEN

Jean waved to Karen as her friend drove off. They'd unlocked the Exhibits building and then Karen had driven her to the only car rental place in town. It didn't take long for Jean to fill out the paperwork and receive the keys to a mid-sized car. "I need to go pick up the ribbons, so I'll need some trunk space and a big back seat," she explained to Karen.

"You don't have to convince me," Karen said as she walked around the car with Jean. They were looking for any damage to document on one of the forms. Jean didn't want to pay for someone else's blunder. She made note of a few scratches and dings but the car was in good shape. Jean signed the forms and turned them over to the clerk. He handed her the keys and she went out to the car.

"That's it, Karen. Thanks for the ride."

"It's no problem, you know that. Are you heading off to get the ribbons now?"

"I am. I called the guy and told him why I had to be late. He understood."

"I wish you'd send someone else."

Jean shrugged. "Everyone else is busy with judging today. You know how that works, I don't, so this is the best thing."

Karen gave her friend a hug and got in her car. "Hope the AC works in that. You're going to need it."

Now Jean was alone in her rental in the rental car parking lot and still hadn't started it up. She watched the traffic on the highway running through the center of town. Cars zipped by the parking lot heading north to cooler weather or south, back to Phoenix. It was hypnotic, watching the cars go by while sitting in the heat of the car. She picked up her cell phone from the center console and speed-dialed her son.

"Hey, Mom," he answered the phone.

"Hi, Jim." It was good to hear his voice.

"Great hearing from you, Mom. Anything wrong? You don't usually call in the middle of the day during work hours."

He's a bright boy. "Yeah, my car was vandalized last night. All the tires were slashed."

"What? Are you all right?"

She could hear the panic and fear in his voice. "I'm fine, Jim. I've already talked to the police and gotten a rental car."

"What happened, Mom? I thought you said that town was safe."

"It's safe enough. I found a body two days ago in the storage container at the fair."

"What? You didn't tell me? Should I come over there?"

Jim lived in Los Angeles and had a good job as a programmer at a major computer company. "That's not necessary, Jim." *Maybe I shouldn't have called him.*

"I'm fine. The body has already been identified and the police are working on the case. Karen and I were curious and went to talk to a guy about his relationship with the dead woman."

"You did *what*?"

Jean sighed. She shouldn't have called him. "We talked to the guy last night. Just to see if he had any information about the woman. Ina was her name."

"For God's sake, Mom. He could have killed you or something. Maybe you should leave the investigating to the police."

In her mind's eye she could see him running a hand through his black hair. That's what he always did when he was upset. He was twenty-five years old but still her son. "Don't get stressed, I'm fine. Give Lisa a kiss for me and big hugs to Rio and Glen, would you?"

"I will, Mom. But please be careful. I'm going to be worried sick until they catch whoever slashed your tires."

"I'll be careful, son. Bye." She clicked off and wiped the trickle of sweat from her temple. She started the car and, after searching the unfamiliar dashboard, turned on the air conditioner. The blast of cold air was a relief. Okay, time to go get ribbons.

CHAPTER NINETEEN

Analise took her hands off of her hips and pointed at Barry, the Vendor Manager for the Fair. It was ten in the morning and already the sun made the midway space a bake-oven. Vendor vehicles were going in every direction, trying to park in their assigned spaces. Analise's gourmet sandwich truck was stopped in the middle of the midway, blocking the path of half of the other vendors. Dust rose around them and made Barry's eyes water. "I'm not taking that spot, Barry Cole. No one comes down that far. Last year I barely made a dime. Give me a different spot."

Cole checked his midway diagram. "Look Analise, your spot is right by the stage. People will be there all day and night till closing. The stage is new. It'll have a lot of people in front of it." He held it out for her to see.

She glanced at the diagram. "Just because you drew a square and called it a stage doesn't mean it's going to have a lot of people in front of it. Why can't I have that spot?" She pointed to the space behind Cole. "It's the middle of the midway, right in the action. Give me that spot."

Cole rubbed his forehead. He could feel the grit of the dust on his face under the sweat. *Why do I volunteer for this every year?* "I have the Knights of Columbus in that spot. They've had that spot for the last twenty years. I'm not going to kick them out of that spot. People look for them there."

Analise tapped her cowboy-booted right foot and crossed her arms. "Don't mess with me, Barry. I'll be in front of the town council so fast you won't know what happened."

Cole clenched his teeth together. He knew what she was doing, threatening his wife who served on the council. Analise had done this before, bringing complaints against local businesspeople who ticked her off. "You can do that if you want, Analise, but not today."

A truck horn sounded. A man stuck his head out of the window of a giant Ford towing a barbeque trailer right behind Analise's truck. "What's going on, Barry? What's the hold-up?"

"Just a little discussion about the space assignment. We'll be done in a second."

"Oh no we won't. If I don't get a different spot, I'm planting my truck right here." Analise spoke loud enough for the barbeque guy to hear.

Another truck sounded its horn, backed up behind the barbeque man.

Barry could feel his blood pressure rising. "You can't hold everyone up, Analise. There's nothing wrong with your spot."

"Get a move on, lady!"

The second truck sounded its horn again.

She crossed her arms, walked back to her truck and leaned against the driver's side door. Cole sighed. He walked over to the barbeque truck and helped the man inch around her, then did the same with the second truck. When they were clear he pulled his phone out of his pocket. He dialed Jean.

"Hello?"

"Jean, it's Barry Cole. I've got an irate vendor who doesn't like her spot and is threatening to block the whole midway if I don't change her location." He could hear a sigh on the other end of the phone.

"I'm at the north end of town. I'll be there in a few."

They clicked off. Fifteen minutes later, Jean walked up to the Vendor Manager. They stared at the sandwich truck, still causing problems in the middle of the midway. "Who's that?"

"Analise Van Horn."

Jean sighed and rolled her eyes. "Wonderful." The noise of the vendors setting up was loud enough that they had to raise their voices to hear each other.

"Yep. I tried to tell her that her spot is right next to the bandstand. It will be busy every day of the fair but she won't listen."

"Show me your diagram," Jean said.

He held out his clipboard. "She wants the Knights of Columbus spot cause it's in the middle. They've had that spot for decades; I don't want to make them move."

"What's this spot?" Jean pointed at a square that didn't have a label on it.

"That's over there." He pointed to the right side of the midway, four spots down from where they stood. "It's a new vendor, selling corn dogs. He's never been here. He signed up at the last minute."

"Give Analise that spot. Put the corn dog guy in her spot. Will that work for you?"

He gave the diagram another look. "Yeah, I can do that. Think she'll go for it?"

"Let's see." Jean and Barry walked over to Analise, still standing in the shade of her truck and glaring at the other vendors.

"Analise," Jean said.

"Jean." Analise stood up. "Have you convinced Cole to give me that spot?" She jerked her chin at the Knights of Columbus space.

"We decided not to do that."

Analise scowled at Cole, then at Jean. Barry was glad Jean was doing the talking. "Instead we have a space on the right, three spots down from here. Take a look."

Analise walked around the front of her truck. Cole and Jean followed. On the right she could see an empty spot between a jewelry vendor and a lemonade stand. She walked over to it and walked around it.

"The lemonade is going to draw flies."

The lemonade vendor shot her a glare, and Barry spoke up before he could say anything. "All of the food vendors will draw flies, Analise. We're outside. It happens."

Analise scowled and looked up and down the midway where every spot had people setting up. "Fine." She uncrossed her arms and strode toward her truck. Jean and Cole walked over to the end of the midway, out of Analise's way. They stopped and watched her pull her truck into the space, the lemonade guy eyeing her every move.

"Don't let the two of them come to blows." Jean

checked her watch.

"I'll talk to the guy. Thanks for helping out. The woman makes me a nervous wreck."

Jean patted him on the shoulder. "Me too. Look, I've got to go get ribbons. Talk with Karen over in the Exhibits building if you need anything."

Cole tucked the clipboard under his arm. "Sure. Drive safe."

"I will." She headed over to the Exhibits building to give Karen a heads-up about Analise before she left.

CHAPTER TWENTY

Nick White pulled into the fairgrounds parking lot and got out of his car. It was just after ten thirty in the morning and the sun was beating down on the asphalt like a punch in the head. He pulled his Stetson out and put it on. It didn't make his head any cooler but it at least cut the glare. The gates were open to allow vendors to come in and set up. Trucks, trailers, cars, golf carts, and four-wheelers were buzzing back and forth, people were yelling, hammers were clanking against poles and wooden boards; it looked and sounded like a zoo.

He spotted Jean Hays in the center of the melee, walking with Analise Van Horn to an empty spot near the fence. *Don't envy her that,* he thought as he locked his car and headed for the gate. *It's no wonder Arris divorced her. What a witch.* After a few moments he watched Jean and a man with a clipboard walk away. He was almost to the gate when he saw her say something to the man, then turn and head away from the midway.

Nick intercepted her at the gate. Her blue eyes were looking straight ahead like a woman on a mission. Her short, graying brown hair was stuck to her temples and forehead with a sheen of sweat. *She's going to get sunburned wearing that sleeveless top and shorts.* "Hi, Ms. Hays."

Jean stopped short and spun around.

Ah, still a little spooked. Recognition spread across her face. He was surprised to see a scowl follow soon after.

"Chief White." The scowl disappeared. "What can I do for you?"

"I thought I'd stop by and say how sorry I am your car was vandalized. We're working the case as fast as we can." A look of suspicion flashed across her face, then resignation.

"I appreciate that, Chief."

"You can call me Nick."

Her right eyebrow rose up. She nodded. "Nick. I appreciate that. I suspect it falls behind the murder though, as far as priorities go."

She's quick. "Yeah, it has to, but we'll work it as fast as we can."

"Any chance I can get my ribbons today? It's judging day. If not, I have to drive to Gila County and get borrowed ribbons."

My God, she's relentless. He scuffed his boot in the dust. "I'm sorry, no. The lab just couldn't work that fast." He admitted to himself that it was a pain for her to have to drive so far and then be indebted to the other fair. "Is it going to cost you much?"

"They're selling us the ribbons at their cost, if that's what you mean. Then there's the time it'll take me to drive there and get back, then go back through all of the exhibits to attach ribbons. Let's call it an inconvenience."

"I'm sorry about that. I really am."

He was surprised to see a tiny smile start on her face. "Well, it's a pain in my ass but we'll have to deal with it. I'm on my way to talk to one of the Superintendents, and then I'll take off for Gila County. Is there anything else?"

That explained her focus as she was walking. *She's got a lot on her plate.* "No. I just wanted to check and make sure you're all right. Let you know you're next on the priority list. I try to talk to everyone that has a serious call into the office."

That made her grin. "Thank you, Chief. I appreciate that."

He tipped his hat. "Drive safe, Ms. Hays."

"You can call me, Jean, Nick." She gave him a wave and turned and walked away. Head was up, shoulders squared, striding right along. Her military training, he thought as he watched her go around the stands of the show ring. He reset his hat and walked out through the gate.

#

At the Exhibits building Jean saw every department deep into the judging. Volunteers were arranging the already judged exhibits. She found Karen, helping a judge with an exhibit. "Karen, I'm sorry to interrupt."

Karen looked up from the judging sheet. "Hi Jean, I thought you'd be gone by now." She turned to the judge. "Can you give me just a minute?"

"Sure," the woman said. "It'll give me time to think

about this one."

Karen stepped over to Jean. "Everything all right?"

Jean waved a hand. "Yeah. I was on my way out of town when Cole called me. Analise was having a fit in the middle of the midway. I had to stop by and solve it. I'm kind of putting you in charge here while I'm gone. I told Barry to talk to you if something comes up. That won't step on anyone's toes, will it?"

"No." Karen shook her head. The VP of Livestock isn't going to want to deal with vendors or plumbing. It'll be okay. Anything else?"

"No. Yeah." Jean wiped at a trickle of sweat that was running down her temple. "I was just stopped by Chief White on my walk here from the vendor area. Wanted to make sure I was all right."

Karen's eyebrows shot up. "He did?"

Jean nodded. "Is that odd or what?"

"Yeah," Karen said slowly, drawing the word out. She grinned. "Think he has a crush on you?"

Jean snorted. "Cold day in hell." She drew a deep breath. "Okay, I'm on my way to Gila County. Hold down the fort."

"I will. Drive safe."

CHAPTER TWENTY-ONE

When Nick left the fairgrounds he drove across the highway to the casino. The smell of cigarettes hit him in the face as he walked through the automatic doors. He wrinkled his nose. He quit smoking when he was twenty-two but the smell still stirred cravings. A casino security guard stood just inside the door. Nick nodded to him as he passed and headed to the casino offices.

He had counted four commercial buses in the parking lot. The slots floor was full of seniors with walkers, canes, and portable oxygen tanks moving from one slot machine to the next. About three quarters of the seats were filled, cigarettes smoldering in ashtrays next to the machines. The noise was enough to drive a man insane. He watched an elderly woman, blank-faced, push a big green button on the face of the machine. Lights flashed, bells rang, but her expression never changed. She just pushed the button again. *I don't get the thrill.*

He left the casino floor and turned down a

carpeted hallway leading to a ballroom area. Halfway along the hall, he turned right into a door marked *Office*. A secretary, a young woman of Apache Indian descent, sat at a desk. "Hi, Chief," she said. Her brown eyes brightened. "We haven't seen you in here in a while. What can we do for you?"

"I need to talk to Jimmy, Lani. He around?"

Lani picked up the office phone and punched a button. "I have Chief White here to see you." She listened a moment. "Sure. I'll send him right back." She hung up.

"He said to go on in. You want some coffee? I'm bringing him some." She stood up.

"No, I'm good, Lani. Thanks." The Chief walked past Lani's desk, a huge printer, and a conference table to an office door to the left. He gave it a quick rap and walked in.

"Nick White, you old dog. Come on in." Dressed in slacks and a white long-sleeved shirt, sleeves rolled to his elbows, Jimmy stood up and came around his modern walnut desk to shake hands. "Haven't seen you in too long."

Nick walked across the plush, sand-colored carpet and shook hands. "You're right. It has been too long. Thanks again for that contribution to the Police Widows fund. It came just in time for Officer Morgan's widow. I appreciate it."

"Glad to help, Nick, you know that. Have a seat. What do you need?" His braid swayed across his back as he sat down in a modern black leather executive chair. "Lani's bringing coffee."

Nick waved the offer off. "I told her none for me, thanks anyway. I'm here about Ina Grange."

Jimmy sighed. "What a shame. We knew her in

school, ahead of us by three years. Such a nice girl."

A knock came on the door and it opened. "Here's your coffee, Jimmy. You sure I can't get you something, Chief?"

"No, thanks, Lani. I appreciate the offer."

Lani nodded and left, closing the door behind her. Nick settled into the matching visitor chair to Jimmy's executive chair. He looked around Jimmy's office. There was a painting, wild horses running across the desert. He nodded at it. "That's new."

Jimmy grinned. "Yeah. I got it at the last art show we had in the ballroom. Local artist painted it. I love the way you can almost hear them thundering across the land."

"Good choice, Jim." He turned back to the task at hand. "I need some info on Ina. I'm hearing she had a gambling problem."

Jimmy had picked up his cup. He hesitated with it halfway to his mouth, then went ahead and took a sip. He placed it carefully on the saucer. "You know we do our best to cooperate with law enforcement, Nick."

Nick relaxed into the chair. He knew that Jimmy had to answer to the casino council, made up of tribe elders. They never liked to reveal information about the casino. "I know you do, Jimmy. I'm just trying to figure out who may have killed Ina."

The casino manager folded his hands on the desk. "I'm limited in what I can share, Nick. You know that."

"I do," Nick acknowledged. "I need to know how much she owed you and how you were collecting."

Jimmy's eyebrows knit together. "You think we were strongarming her? You know better than that."

"I don't think you were strongarming her, Jimmy. I do know you better than that."

Jimmy's scowl softened. "She owed us a lot, Nick. We sent the debt to a collection agency. The tribe doesn't want any trouble with the Gaming Commission or the town. We're good neighbors here."

"You are that. The town appreciates it." Nick sat forward, elbows on knees. "But I need to know who else she might have owed money to that might not be as nice."

Jimmy rocked back in his chair. "I don't know, Nick. She played the ponies, sometimes. Maybe someone from the track? But the season doesn't start here in Arizona for another couple of months. It's too hot yet for horse racing."

Nick scratched his head. "I was hoping you would know where else I could look."

"I'm sorry, Nick. Really I am. I feel bad about her murder."

Nick thought hard. "How about a print-out of her member card activity? Can you give me that?"

Jimmy stared at the wall behind Nick and rubbed his chin. "Yeah," he agreed with misgiving plain on his face. "I think I can get the elders to approve that. Can I send it over to your office after I talk to them?"

"Sure." Nick was pleased with the concession. A thought crossed his mind. "Ina never was in a ruckus in here was she? A yelling match? Anything?"

The manager's head did a slow shake as he thought about it. "Noooo," he drew out the word. "Oh, wait." He rocked forward in the chair. "A few months ago, she was on a winning streak and some guy was trying to get her to cash out." He tugged at his left ear. "I don't remember much else so security must have busted the commotion up pretty fast."

This might be a clue. Nick leaned forward. "You have any record? Logs? Video?"

Jim's hand hit the executive phone on his desk. "Lani," he said when the young woman picked up. "Tell security to do a log search on Ina Grange, um, past nine months. Any video from that time, too."

"Sure thing," Nick heard over the intercom. She clicked off.

"I'll have to clear this with the elders, too, ya know." Jimmy rocked back in his chair.

"That's fine, I can wait a bit. This won't get you in trouble, will it?"

"I don't think so. The elders are careful to protect the tribe but where this kind of thing happens, they want to be on the side of the law."

Nick stood up. "Thanks for seeing me, Jimmy." He paused. "Oh, I had a report that shortly before her disappearance, a couple of the tribe were seen leaving her house. Any idea what that was about?"

Jimmy's face became passive. "No, no idea. Like I said, we use collection agencies."

"Had to ask. Thanks for the help."

"Any time, Nick." Jimmy stood up and walked Nick to the door. "Let me know if there's anything else we can do." He opened his office door. "I'm serious. Anything at all. A reward even, if you think that will help."

They shook hands. "I appreciate that, Jimmy. Thanks."

CHAPTER TWENTY-TWO

Jean met Arris's friend in Gila County and picked up four totes full of ribbons, everything from the green Merit ribbons to the Best of Show ribbons.

"Tell Arris I'm sorry about his troubles. My wife and I met the woman, Ina, once when Arris drove over for a barbeque at my house. Lovely lady, but they argued."

Jean perked her ears.

He waved his hand. "Nothin' violent. It just seemed like she wanted something and Arris said no. 'We're staying here.' His exact words."

"Did it cause a problem?"

"Nope. They stayed the day, then drove home that night. They seemed okay when they left."

"When was this?"

"Oh…" The man took off his cowboy hat and scratched his head. "About October last year. Just after the weather cooled off enough to have a nice picnic."

"Well, thank you for the ribbons." Jean needed

time to puzzle out whether this information would be worth anything or not.

A bill accompanied the totes. Fair enough, Jean thought when the guy handed it to her. She tucked it into her shorts pocket and shook his hand. "I appreciate it. I'll tell Arris hello for you."

She got in her car and looked at the dashboard clock. "Four ten now, two-hour drive back. Ummm, I'll stop at a drive-thru before I leave town. I can call Karen and tell her I'll be there at about seven. She can tell everyone else and we can get the exhibits their ribbons before midnight." She sighed with a bit of satisfaction and started the car. Jean was in the drive-thru line when her phone rang.

"Hi."

"Ms. Hays, this is Nick White."

Uh oh, he's back to calling me Ms. Hays. Something must be wrong. "Chief. Something wrong?"

"Yes, very wrong. Did you and Karen Carver go see Josh Marlow last night?"

Her heart sank. "Yeah."

"You can't do that." It sounded as though he were gritting his teeth.

"I can't talk to people?"

"You can't go around conducting your own investigation into Ina Grange's death."

"We heard he knew her, that's all." Jean made an effort to make it less than it was. The car ahead of her pulled forward. She inched up behind it.

"He filed stalking charges." Nick's voice was flat.

Oh no. This was bad. "He did?"

"Yes, and I don't blame him."

Jean's hand went slick on her cell phone. "What happens now?"

She heard him draw a deep breath. "Nothing about the stalking charges, I talked him down. But I promised him you wouldn't approach him again."

Jean slumped with relief. "Thank you, Chief White. I appreciate it."

"You aren't off the hook, Ms. Hays. I want to know why you were out there."

She inched the car forward again. "We heard that Josh had dated Ina before Arris. We just thought we'd ask him if he knew of anyone that would want to hurt her." *Is he going to buy this excuse?*

He snorted. "You thought no such thing. You were thinking he might be a suspect, jealousy maybe."

Jean rolled her eyes. *He's got us for sure.* "A little of that," she admitted. Her hand was wet on the steering wheel despite the car's air conditioning.

"You could have been killed, way out there in the middle of nowhere. Is that what you want?"

I wish everyone would stop saying that. "No, Chief." Now she was getting angry. He was treating her like a dummy. She gripped the phone harder. "I was just trying to help Arris."

"That's my job, Ms. Hays. Unless you'd like to be charged with interfering in a police investigation, you need to back off. Is that understood?"

"Yes, Chief White. I understand." She heard him click off. A horn behind her startled her. She was two car lengths behind the vehicle in front of her. She waved an apology and pulled up. *Perfect, now he thinks I'm an interfering nut job. I wonder if he called Karen and read her the riot act, too.* Her fingers tapped on the steering wheel. *I wonder if he was even looking at Josh Marlow. Killing someone and stuffing them in a cabinet that Arris controls sounds like the work of a jealous lover to me.*

It was her turn to order. "Burger and fries. Iced tea, please."

She pulled up behind the car in front of her at the delivery window. *I don't believe for a minute that Arris is the murderer.* What about the gambling? Arris didn't have anything to do with that. What about Vera and Analise? *Does Mr. High and Mighty Chief White know about that?* She fumed until she pulled up to the window. Jean handed over the cash and got her drink and the bag. She thanked the girl and pulled out. It wasn't until she was out on the highway that she opened the bag. One-handed she unwrapped the burger and bit into it as though it were an enemy.

CHAPTER TWENTY-THREE

It was a little after six in the evening when Karen put dinner on the table. Peggy had invited her boyfriend, Tyler, to eat with them. "Help yourself, Tyler," she said as she put the coleslaw on the table.

"Thank you, Karen. It looks good."

Spread out on the table, in addition to the coleslaw, were grilled pork chops, fresh green beans and a bowl of rice. Tyler picked up the coleslaw and put a spoonful on his plate. "How goes the fair business?" He passed the bowl to Peggy.

"Good. Judging finished today." Karen shook her head. "Poor Jean had to drive all the way to Gila County to get ribbons from their fair. We all have to go in about seven to put ribbons on all the exhibits that earned one."

"That sucks, Mom. You just got home!"

"True, but we want everyone to see how well they did. It's not really a fair if there are no ribbons." She speared a pork chop and put it on her plate, then passed the rest to Tyler.

"Don't people give back the ribbons?" Peggy passed the green beans to her mother.

"They do?" Tyler looked up from the pork chops in surprise.

"Some do." Karen took some green beans and passed the bowl. "Mostly the people who enter every year. They don't really want to keep the ribbons, they'd be overwhelmed if they did. So they enjoy them on their exhibits and on Sunday they'll remove them and give them back. A lot of people give back their premiums, too. A donation to the fair."

"Wow, they give back the prize money?" Tyler put the green bean bowl on the table after helping himself.

"It's not that much, really," Karen told them. "And it helps the fair."

"So who's running the fair if Jean has been gone all day?" Peggy asked over a forkful of beans.

"I have. And I'm glad to help. Her car tires were slashed last night."

"Oh no." Peggy stopped eating. "She wasn't hurt, was she?"

Karen looked at both of them, staring across the table. "No, but a warning was scrawled across her windshield." She saw Tyler swallow, then sip his tea.

"What did it say?" he asked.

"Stop investigating." She watched Tyler closely. *Does he know something?*

"I told you it was a bad idea to go see Josh Marlow, Mom." Peggy cut into her chop. "You could have been killed."

"You think Josh killed Ina?" Tyler picked up his fork and stirred the coleslaw on his plate.

Karen raised an eyebrow. "I don't know." She

picked up her fork and skewered a green bean. "But Chief White called me today. Josh tried to file a stalking complaint against me and Jean. The Chief talked him out of it."

"Oh my God, Mom!"

Tyler stared again.

"It's all taken care of, don't worry."

"Mom, are you going to be safe?"

"Of course I am." Karen calmly ate another bit of pork chop. "Nothing is going to happen." She finished off her coleslaw and got up to rinse off her plate.

"Leave that, Mom. You have to go back to the fairgrounds. Tyler and I will take care of the dishes."

Karen rinsed off her plate and put it beside the sink. "Thank you, Peg. I appreciate that." She wiped her hands on the tea towel. "That lets me get there early and get the paperwork ready so we can attach ribbons quickly." She gave her daughter a kiss on the head. "Hopefully we won't be working too late."

"I hope so, Mom."

Karen left the kitchen, wondering if Marlow had been the tire slasher. She heard Peggy laugh. When she turned to look, Peg was talking to Tyler and picking up the dishes. Tyler was watching Karen.

CHAPTER TWENTY-FOUR

Jean had the security guard open the gate so she could drive up to the middle door of the Exhibits building. Before Jean had the trunk open, Karen was at the driver's side door. "You made it!"

Jean laughed. "Yeah, nothing like a road trip to save the day."

Three of the other Superintendents showed up at the trunk. They each grabbed a tote. "The last one is in the back seat," Jean told Karen as she closed the trunk.

"I'll take it in. You go park."

"Thanks, Karen." She held the door as Karen removed the tote. "I'll be back in a sec."

After she parked the car she helped the security guard, Sam, shut and lock the big gate. "Has there been any trouble, Sam?"

"Not a bit, Jean. I walked around in here all night last night, nothing going on. I even check the parking lot once in awhile. Isn't that a new car?"

"A rental. Someone slashed the tires on my car last

night."

He eyed her. "Hence the questions about my night." He put the chain and padlock on the fence gate and snapped it shut. "I'll keep an extra eye out."

"Thanks, Sam." Jean smiled. "I'd hate anything to happen to people's prized possessions while they're under my care."

"I'll take care, Jean."

"Appreciate it, Sam."

She waved and walked to the Exhibits building. The heat of the day had dissipated, and it was about eighty degrees. The sky was so clear the Milky Way was easily visible. It seemed as though she could just reach up and scoop a handful of stars out of the sky. She could smell the livestock but it was far enough away that it wasn't unpleasant. The cattle were mooing softly and she could hear the 4-H and FFA kids laughing over the sound of music playing. She almost hated having to go into the Exhibits building.

When she did, it was a hive of quiet activity. Every Superintendent was reading off of their exhibit records while one volunteer found the exhibit and another tied on the appropriate ribbon. She grabbed a bottle of water from the cooler. It was full. Karen must have refilled it, she thought as she unscrewed the top and drank half of it down. She'd dehydrated during the afternoon. She didn't want to stop for bathroom breaks more than necessary. She watched another minute while she finished the bottle off, dropped the bottle it in the trash bag and wiped her hands on her shorts.

Jean had taken three steps when she heard her name from the doorway. Spooked, she spun around.

It was Nick White, Stetson in hand. "Oh, sorry,

Ms. Hays. I didn't mean to startle you." He scuffed his feet on the cement floor.

Her heart was racing. She waved off the apology. "That's okay. I just didn't expect anyone to come in behind me." She swallowed the fear that had surged through her. He really did look apologetic. "Is there a problem, Chief?"

He came inside the building, looking around at everyone working. "It's busy in here."

"Yeah." She wiped her hands on her shorts again. "I just got back with the ribbons. Everyone are being troopers and staying late to get them attached."

He nodded. She could see his blue eyes taking in every detail. "Uh, I just stopped by to let you know we're still working on your case. The car has been fingerprinted and the prints entered into a database search."

"That's good." She looked over in the direction of Karen's department. Karen was busy and never looked toward the door. She smiled at him. "Can my car be released?"

"Not yet," he said as he turned his hat in his hands. She watched the hat go around and around. "Sorry about that."

She shrugged. "It'll take as long as it takes. You know a good tire place? I'm going to have to get new ones."

He brightened. "Go to Tire Palace, over on Round Up Road off of Arrow Highway. Ask for Andy Jenkins. Tell him I sent you over and he'll give you a good price."

"Thanks, Chief." She smiled at him. "I'll give him a call."

"I spoke to the security guard, Sam, when I came

in. Good guy. Spent some time in Iraq."

"Yes, he is a good guy."

"I just wanted to make sure everything in here is okay."

Her right eyebrow went up. *Is he checking on me?* "I promise I'm not talking to Josh Marlow, Chief."

He looked surprised. "Oh, no, I didn't mean that. I mean," he blushed, "I just wanted to be sure there were no problems over here. I mean, you were attacked last night."

She noticed the hat spun faster in his hands. "Everything in here seems good, Chief." He was confusing her. This afternoon he was chewing her out. Tonight he was all concerned. "Uh, I thought we were on a first-name basis?"

He blushed a brighter shade of red. "Uh, yeah." He stepped to the center aisle and looked down to the far end of the building where the Gems and Minerals department was. "Yes, Jean. We are."

"Good to know, Nick."

"I see John down there, let me go say hello." He put his hat on, tipped it to her slightly, turned on his heel and strode off along the center of the building.

She snorted and shook her head. Karen showed up beside her. "Chief White checking on us?"

"I think so," Jean chuckled. "Or me, anyway."

"Hoo, hoo, hoo! Do I detect a little romance in the air?"

"Not likely." Jean turned to her friend. "Need any more help?"

"Sure, one of my volunteers has to go. You can help me finish up."

Two hours later Karen gave Jean her exhibits sheets. "Here you go. I'm glad you have to tally all this stuff up and not me."

"You had to tally up your department's prize totals." Jean grinned at her.

"Yeah, but not everything in the building. Don't stay too late." Karen moved toward the door.

"I won't. Photography is nearly done. I have a calculator in my bag. I'll start working on everyone else's. By the time they turn their sheets in, I'll be nearly done."

"Okay. I'm going home, take a shower and fall into bed. Opening is at eight and I want to get a little sleep anyway."

"Have a good night."

Jean cleared one corner of an exhibit stand and spread out the paperwork. Each department made note of how many exhibits were entered by seniors, by adults and by juniors, 17 years old or less. They also had to keep track of all the prizes that were awarded in each department. Merit awards earned no premiums. White, or third place, earned a dollar. Red, or second place, earned two dollars and first-place Blue earned three dollars. Other awards, such as Judge's Choice or Best in Class or Best of Show won only bragging rights. No extra prize money was awarded for those ribbons. She dug out a sheet of paper and starting making notes by department. By the time she had it all down, the Photography Superintendent, Ernie Hale, was walking up to her.

"Here ya go, Jean. Sorry it took so long. We had about two hundred more entries this year than last."

"That's okay, Ernie. I'm just now getting to your department."

"Don't stay too much longer, Jean. It's after ten already."

"I won't be long, Ernie. I have to get your numbers, add everything up and I'll be done. I can turn it in to the treasurer in the morning."

He waved as he left the building. It took her another half hour to add his numbers to her list, add it all up and double-check it. She filled out the form she needed to give the treasurer. Jean filed everything away and tucked it all under the display stand. She'd pull it out and give it to Mason Brown in the morning. The Livestock VP did the numbers for that side of the house. Everything tidied up, she stretched. Sitting in the car all day and then hunched over paperwork for an hour was doing her back no favors. After turning off the fans, she got her purse, grabbed the trash bag and made a mental note to bring more water in the morning. One more look around and she turned off the lights and locked the door. On the way to the gate, she dropped her trash in a handy trash barrel. They were already set up for the fair opening in the morning.

Sam was at the gate. "I heard your fans go off so I came over to let you out."

"Thanks Sam. Have a good night."

"I will, Jean. Be careful out there."

"I will. We appreciate you doing this for us."

"Not a problem. I like the quiet out here."

"Good night."

"Night."

He locked the gate behind her and she could hear his boots crunching away toward the livestock area. Nice guy, she thought as she approached her car. It was parked about a hundred feet away from the gate, as close as parking could get. She dug the keys out of her pocket and, fifty feet away from the car, hit the button on the remote to unlock the vehicle. The parking and brake lights flashed. In the stillness she could hear the locks disengage.

She was tired, her back hurt from sitting in the car for hours and all she wanted was a hot shower, a glass of wine while she checked her email, and bed. She opened the back door to put her tote bag in the back seat. She took a step to the front door and was reaching out for the handle when she heard footsteps crunching on loose gravel behind her. Her heart sped up and she spun around. She had a glimpse of a man, all in black, with his hand raised. That's the last she remembered.

CHAPTER TWENTY-FIVE

Jean woke in a hospital bed, arm tethered to an IV, her head splitting with pain. She reached up to touch her head; her arm felt as though it had lead weights on it. She could feel a bandage, and it was sore and tender on the left side. The lights were dim and she could hear the heart monitor beeping. What she wanted more than information was a drink of water. A bed-stand stood against the wall. While she was eyeing it and wondering if she could get out of bed and get a glass of water, a nurse bustled in.

"Ah, you're awake, good." The woman viewed the monitor and tapped a button. The beeping stopped.

"Thanks for that," Jean croaked. "I'd be crazy in another few minutes."

"I heard it speed up, that's how I knew you were awake." The woman fluffed up the pillows and tapped a note in the computer pad in her pocket. "I'm Becky. What can I get you?"

"Water. My mouth feels nasty."

The nurse bustled over to the stand, grabbed the

water pitcher and a glass and disappeared into the bathroom to fill it. She stuck her head around the corner. "Do you want ice?"

"No, not now." Jean shifted to pull the bedgown down; it had bunched up under her back.

The nurse put the water on the table and wheeled it over to the bed. "Can you reach this?"

Jean grabbed the glass carefully, her arms still felt like lead. "I can, thanks. Can you tell me what happened?"

The nurse's eyebrow twitched and she reached into the pocket where she had tucked the pad. "What do you remember?"

"I locked up the Exhibits building, said good night to Sam," she looked up at the nurse. "He's the Security Guard at the Fair. Then walked to my car. I had just put my bag in the car and was reaching for the driver door handle when I heard someone coming up behind me. I turned around and," she took a breath, "that's all I remember."

"You don't remember anything else?"

Jean slowly shook her head. Any rapid movement made her head hurt. "No, well, it was a man. That's it."

"You were brought in about midnight. You have a three-inch gash in your scalp but the skull wasn't broken. You probably have a concussion. Is there anyone we can call for you?"

"No. My son lives in LA. I can call him in the morning."

Becky nodded. "Okay. The police are outside, they want to question you about what happened."

"That's fine, send them in."

"Let me know if you need anything." Becky drew

the cord with the call button around the head of the bed and looped it around the rail on Jean's right. "So it doesn't slip away."

She left the room. Jean took a deep breath and winced when the skin on her scalp stretched. Her eyes went wide when she saw Nick White step into the room. He pulled his Stetson off. "Jean."

"Nick. We seem to be seeing a lot of each other lately."

His step faltered. It was a moment before he recovered. "Seems so. Can you tell me what happened?"

She shared what she had told the nurse.

"You recognize the guy? White guy? Black guy? How tall?"

The parking lot was dark. He was covered in black." She closed her eyes and took a deep breath, wincing again. "At least I think it was black, hard to tell. He had gloves on and a ski mask, just his eyes showing. White." She opened her eyes. "He was white, a little skin showed. But it was too dark to see his eye color."

Nick was jotting notes in a small paper notebook. "Anything else?"

She raised her left hand to touch the bandage over the gash. "He was right-handed."

He nodded.

"How do you feel?"

"Like I've been clubbed." She drank half a glass of water. "I'm thirsty, too. I don't know why the air in hospitals is always so dry."

"It's the drugs. They make you thirsty." He eyed her. "Have you been doing anymore investigating?"

A wash of anger swept over her. "No." Her tone

109

was snippy. "I spent half of yesterday on the road. Then I was at the fair, as you well know. Then I tried to go home."

He raised a hand to calm her. "I had to ask. Someone has it out for you."

"Sorry." She rubbed the bridge of her nose. "I guess I'm a little annoyed right now."

"I can understand that." He scuffed a boot on the floor tile. "I just need you to leave it alone. Someone thinks you're investigating or know something. Leave the investigating to me. Can you take a vacation or go somewhere for a few days?"

"No. With Arris out of the picture, I'm the one running the fair. I've got to get out of here in the morning and get back to it." She could see his jaw working in his tanned face.

"Maybe so. Just be careful. I'll let you rest." He tipped his hat and walked out of the room.

Jean poured herself another glass of water and drank it down. *Face it, Jean. You are a little scared. This was the second attack on you.* Her arms felt a little better and she fingered the wounded area on her head. She explored above and below the bandage. A sigh of disgust escaped her. *I'll bet they shaved my hair off. Damn it. I'll have to wear a scarf.* She let her hand fall down to the bed and she looked around the room. Now that she was aware, it seemed too light to sleep. She pushed the call button.

After a few minutes, Becky came in. "You rang?"

Jean smiled at the joke. "Can you turn off the lights? I'm going to try and get some sleep."

"Good idea. Let me arrange some things." She went to the monitor and touched a few buttons. Then she checked the IV. "This should run till six, we'll be bringing meds around by then anyway. You want the table next to the bed?"

"Yes. I can get a drink if I want."

"Okay." She straightened it up at the side of the bed. "Are you ready?"

"Yeah." Jean turned on her right side and tried to get comfortable. "Thanks."

Becky stopped at the door to check the room one more time. "Ring if you need something." She turned off the lights and closed the room door.

Jean punched the pillow to get it comfortable under her head. *What a day. Hope someone can unlock the building doors in the morning.* She closed her eyes and tried to sleep.

CHAPTER TWENTY-SIX

Nick rang the bell at the coroner's office door in the Greyson Medical Center basement. He'd had about four hours sleep and the smell of formaldehyde and cleaning chemicals was making his first cup of coffee churn in his stomach. The door buzzed open.

The coroner's clerk smiled at him. "Morning, Chief."

"Morning, Candy." *How the hell can she be so chipper first thing in the morning?* "Your boss texted me he has some results."

"Sure thing, Chief. Go on back. He's in theater two."

She turned back to her computer monitor and began clicking away on the keyboard. He strode along the beige, highly waxed floor tiles. The rest of the hall was sterile white. His footsteps echoed along the hall in front of him. He stopped at the door marked *Theater Two* and pushed open the doors.

In front of him was the exam table. The dried corpse of Ina lay on it, draped in surgical towels. That

112

was a bit of a relief; he didn't want to see someone he knew cut all open. The big surprise was that the body didn't smell, at least not too much. Brian Long, the coroner, was standing beside the table, peering through a magnifying glass on a long arm hovered over her body. The body cabinets were housed in another room of the morgue. This room was strictly for autopsies. Various surgical paraphernalia crowded the shelves on the walls, and the table where bodies were washed was to the right of the door. "Hey, Brian."

The doctor looked up. "Hey there, Nick. Come on in." He adjusted the magnifying glass to position it over the corpse's head.

Nick stood beside but just behind the doctor. "What have you got, Brian?"

"We finished the autopsy last night. I had to bring in a specialist from the FBI office in Phoenix. I just didn't have the expertise. And your man, Paul Oliver, was the witness." He adjusted the magnifying glass once more. "Anyway, you can see here," he pointed with a stylus and stood aside a little so Nick could see, "the skull has an indentation, round, about half an inch deep. She was hit pretty hard."

"Is that the cause of death?"

"We couldn't determine that conclusively but that's the likely cause. There was dried blood on the skin, a lot, since it was a scalp wound, but not sufficient to bleed out. There was minimal blood in the cabinet and none in the conex."

So Ina hadn't been killed in the cabinet or on the site. Nick had guessed as much. "I was thinking the body would smell." Nick got close enough to see what the doc was pointing at, then stepped back half a step.

"No, the high heat of the container dried the body, so there wasn't a lot of decomp odor. I read the statement of the person who found the body. She thought it was the smell of dead mice." He looked thoughtful. "I can see where she'd think that. Like the smell of a garden shed that's been closed up for a couple of weeks." He shook himself. "Anyway, the FBI guy showed me how to get the prints from the body. A fascinating method, to be honest. You just—"

Nick interrupted the doctor before too much information was shared. His stomach was still rolling from the smells in the morgue. "Ah, I'm sure, Brian. But what about other injuries? Drugs? Anything?"

Brian stopped his recitation. "Yeah. So, no other injuries. Toxicology came back clean except for alcohol in the bloodstream. She wasn't drunk, though I'd guess she'd had two drinks."

Nick was disappointed. He'd hoped there would be something to go on. "What about the head injury. Any idea what caused it?"

"The FBI guy and I talked about that." The doctor pushed the magnifying glass up and stripped off his gloves. "Our guess is that some sort of ball-peen hammer was used. A small one, ball about an inch in diameter."

Nick scratched his cheek. Those kinds of hammers were used for metal-working. Maybe the thing a ranch hand might need on occasion. "Uh, thanks, Doc." The two men shook hands. "That's helpful."

Nick left the morgue and walked to his car. He had some things to, do but then he had an interview to conduct.

CHAPTER TWENTY-SEVEN

After the six am IV-bag change, Jean took a chance and got up to use the bathroom. She was tired. Even with the door to her room closed, noises from other patients calling out, room doors closing, and nurses' voices echoing up and down the hall had jerked her awake every time she'd fallen asleep.

She managed to guide the IV stand to the bathroom without tripping over the hose. It was helpful, actually, as she could steady herself. Getting out of bed had made her dizzy. The nurse checked on her after about five minutes.

"You doing okay in there?" Becky called through the door.

"Yep. Just washing my hands." Jean wiped her hands on the paper towels and opened the bathroom door. "All done."

"Good. You need help back to the bed?"

"No, the dizziness has passed. I'm getting hungry, actually." Jean shuffled to the bed and eased into it.

Becky rolled the IV stand to a convenient spot. "I

get off in about half an hour. Breakfast is in an hour. Doctors make rounds after breakfast."

"Two more hours? I feel good, can't I leave now?"

Becky frowned. "You had a big hit on your head. The doc is going to want to examine you to be sure you aren't suffering from a concussion or worse."

A sigh escaped from Jean. "Okay. I guess I can wait." An idea sprang into her mind. "Where is my phone? I can make a couple of calls while I wait."

"Um, well, technically, you shouldn't be making cell phone calls from inside the hospital. But…" She walked over to a narrow vertical door in the unit that held the TV and opened it. "Here's your phone." She handed Jean a plastic bag with her name taped across the front.

"Thank you, Becky. I appreciate it. I want to call my son."

Becky tugged the bottom hem of her scrub top down. "Okay. I've got to go. Nice to meet you."

"Nice to meet you too, Becky. You've been very helpful and I appreciate it."

The nurse left. Jean pulled the phone out of the baggie and wished desperately for a cup of hot tea. She drank some water and speed-dialed Karen.

"Hi, Jean. I'm just about to leave for the fairgrounds. What's up?"

"I was attacked last night, Karen. I'm in the hospital."

"Oh my God, Jean! What happened, are you all right?"

"I was whacked in the head, got a gash, but otherwise I'm fine. With any luck I'll be out of here by, oh, I don't know, ten, maybe. I just wondered if you want to stop by and get the building key?"

"Attacked! What is going on?"

Jean could hear things slamming and banging on Karen's end of the phone. "I don't know. Chief White was in here at zero dark thirty asking me questions. I forgot to ask him how I ended up in the hospital."

"What'd he tell you?"

"He didn't tell me much, but he asked if we'd been doing any more investigating. I'll bet he thinks someone thinks we know more than we do."

Jean could hear a door banging in the background. "I'm on my way over. Do you know what room you're in?"

"No, I don't know. Someone should be able to tell you. I've never been in this hospital. I don't even know what street it's on."

Karen laughed. "I'll figure it out. See you in a bit."

"Bye."

She clicked off and took a deep breath. It was time to call her son. She hit the speed dial for him. It was quarter to seven; he might be on his morning commute already. The phone clicked and he answered. "Hello?"

"Hi Jim, it's Mom."

"Hi Mom. I'm on the road. Pretty early for a call, are you okay?"

Jean clicked her tongue. She didn't want to give him bad news while he was driving. "I had a little trouble last night. I'm in the hospital with a scalp wound." She held her breath.

She could hear the road noise in the background. "What happened, Mom?" His voice was tight.

"Not sure, actually. I was attacked in the fairgrounds parking lot last night. I'm fine. I'll be getting out of the hospital this morning."

"For God's sake, Mom. I thought you weren't going to investigate that murder anymore!"

"I didn't. I was busy all day yesterday. I never talked to a soul about it."

"Are you sure you want to stay in that town? Sounds like a piss-poor place."

"The town is nice, Jim. It's actually the first time in decades the town has had a murder. I like it here. The weather is great, I have friends. It's a good place."

She could hear him sigh on the other end. "Okay, Mom. But first it's your tires, now it's you. Somebody's out to get you."

The realization of her situation hit her. A shiver of fear ran down her spine. Maybe it was just bravado yesterday and shock this morning but Jim was right. Someone *was* out to get her. The tires were one thing, but now this was really personal. No wonder the Police Chief was in her room in the middle of the night. She was single-handedly driving up the crime stats in Greyson. "Well, I don't know anything. I'll keep an eye out. "

Jim sighed. "Take care of yourself, Mom. Do I need to come out there? It's only a few hours away."

"Don't do that, Jim. I'm fine."

"Fine. But you call me immediately if something else happens."

"I will, son. Have a good day at work. Drive safe."

He laughed. "I will, Mom." He clicked off.

She hit the disconnect button. *He fine'd me.* She sighed. *My son fine'd me.* She put the phone on the side table that Becky had positioned next to the bed. *Maybe he's right. Someone is out to get me. Who could it be? I talked to Ari and to that Josh Marlow. It can't be Ari, he's*

Karen's cousin. Could our casual questions have made Josh Marlow nervous? As far as I know Nick hasn't questioned him yet. But the police have questioned Arris. Twice. Her head ached and through the ache a new thought started niggling at Jean.

What if it is Arris? Does he know Karen and I are asking around? Arris knows where I live. He knows what car I drive. The injury on her head throbbed and she put her hand over the spot to get it to stop.

She was still pondering that question when the breakfast tray came in.

CHAPTER TWENTY-EIGHT

Jean took a cab to her house after the doctor released her. She had to wear her bloody clothing home so the first thing she did when she got home was toss them in the trash and take a shower. The shower was tricky. She wasn't supposed to let the water hit her head, but her hair was bloody and sticky and she wanted to get it clean. It finally occurred to her to wash her hair in the kitchen sink. She unwrapped the bandage that wrapped around her head and using the sink hose, washed the hair the ER staff hadn't shaved off. Hair clean, she went back to the bathroom and took a look in the mirror.

"Oh my God, did they have to shave so much off?" She turned her head in the mirror. "I look like friggin' Frankenstein's monster!" A three-inch cut went from the top of her head slanting toward the back of her ear. Black stitches pulled the edges together with stitch ends sticking up. She felt them; they were stiff. The skin around the wound was stained orange-brown. Jean shook her head.

"Wonderful."

"Where's the first-aid stuff?" she asked herself. She hadn't needed it since she moved in. After searching three drawers in the sink console, she found the sterile pads and gauze bandages. Using cotton balls she dabbed antiseptic cream on the wound, placed a gauze pad over it and wrapped her head with the bandage. She shook her head. "I look like a mummy."

After she washed her hands she dug around in her dresser for the scarves she had but never wore. She selected one in plain light blue and wrapped it around her head. A button-up-the-front blouse, in a nearly matching blue, eliminated the need to pull a shirt over her bandaged head. Shorts, white ankle socks and sneakers completed her wardrobe change. She felt so much better now that she was clean and in fresh clothing.

In the kitchen she had just picked up her phone to call the cab company when the front doorbell rang.

Chief White was at the door. "Nick!"

"Jean. The hospital told me you were released."

"Uh, yeah. Come on in."

He pulled his hat off and stepped inside. Jean closed the door behind him. "I was about to call a cab."

"A cab?"

She looked at him. "A cab, to take me to the fairgrounds." She stopped short and stared at him. "I assume my rental car is still there?"

"Yes. It's still there. I had the lab do a quick fingerprint check. The rental company said they'd just detailed the car. Aside from the rental reps your prints were the only ones on it, so we left it there."

121

Jean breathed a sigh of relief. "Oh good. I don't know what I'd tell the rental people if it had been taken in for processing."

"You're feeling all right?" A look of confusion, then sheepishness crossed his face. "I mean, you're okay to go work the fair?"

"I'm good enough. I'll take it easy. It's not right to leave the whole thing to Karen and the other Superintendents. They have enough to do." She watched him nod.

"I suppose, but I'm a little concerned about the attack on you." He drew a breath. "We haven't caught whoever did it." He rubbed his face. She could see he hadn't had much sleep.

"I'm sorry, Chief, uh, Nick. I don't know who would think I have any information. If I hear something, I'll let you know but I've already told you everything I got from Josh Marlow and he was the only one I've talked to." She remembered Karen's comments from Wednesday. "Well, there might be something else."

His eyebrows rose. "Something else?"

"It's not much. Ina was known to be in a fierce competition with a Vera MacIlroy in the quilt department. I guess comments were pretty heated last year when Ina won Best of Show. Vera spit on Ina's quilt."

Nick blinked. "Quilt wars?"

His tone of voice made her feel stupid. "Sorry. But Analise got all over me on Tuesday at Ingram's and then Wednesday, Karen mentioned the ongoing feud between those two." She could feel her face heat up. "Anyway, it's a clue, or line of investigation, or whatever."

She walked into the kitchen to get her bag with fair notebook, cell phone, and purse. He followed her, looking around at the living room, pictures of her in uniform, pictures of her son, and friends on the walls. There were a few pieces of southwestern art, pottery, rock drawings and the like on shelves and over the fireplace on the mantle.

"It seems you've settled in pretty well."

She walked back into the living room, keys in hand, bag over her shoulder. "Pretty well. Something I learned while I was in the military. Unpack, get out your belongings, make the place your home." Jean was glad he'd dropped the conversation about quilt wars. It sounded stupid even to her.

He twisted the hat in his hands. "I really wish you'd reconsider going to the fairgrounds. It's dangerous."

Jean adjusted the bag on her shoulder and stared him straight in the eyes. "I made a commitment, Chief, to the fair. It's more than just a cute thing. The county fair is where the members of the community gather to share their skills. Skills, I may remind you, that are rapidly dying out. This is our opportunity to interest the young in these crafts. Not just knitting or quilting, but wood-working, soap-making, growing and preserving food." She pointed at him. "These are life skills, as important, no, more important than how to use a computer. These skills will keep people alive if, God forbid, something horrible happens. Sure, there are bragging rights for raising a prize-winning steer, or running a barrel race on your mustang pony, but more important is the sharing of skills. I will not let the fair falter because I'm a wimp and can't put up with a little headache."

Nick backed up a step at her intensity. He held up his hands in surrender. "Okay, okay. I understand. This is important to you." He grinned at her. "May I offer you a ride to the fairgrounds?"

She took a breath and reset the bag on her shoulder. "Sorry. I get a little passionate." She grinned back at him. "Yes, I'd love a ride to the fair."

He tipped his hat and walked to the door. "Your ride awaits, ma'am."

Jean followed him to the door. "Thank you, sir."

CHAPTER TWENTY-NINE

The ride to the fairgrounds was quiet. Nick didn't know what to say to the woman. He admired her passion for the fair, though. He'd expected her to be one of those women who didn't cook and didn't know anything about doing things for herself. Instead she seemed to be well aware of the ongoing and rapid loss of the skills necessary for survival. He liked that. The lines of an old country and western song ran through his mind. Something about not wanting a drugstore woman, if he remembered correctly. He snuck a glance at her. She wasn't a drugstore woman.

Jean was letting her short hair go gray. There was very little makeup on her face. Little lines were forming at the corners of her eyes. No nonsense, practical, he thought to himself. Her ex must be a fool.

He let her off at the fair gate. "Take care, Jean," he said as she got out.

She leaned in the door. "I will, Nick."

He watched as she went through the gate and

turned to go to the Exhibits building until she was out of sight. Nick glanced at the clock. He had a little while before he had things to do so he picked up the radio and called his friend, Paul Oliver, to meet for coffee.

#

Paul walked through the door of the Highway Diner ten minutes after the call. Nick was already there with a cup of coffee in front of him and the newspaper spread out on the table. Paul called out to the waitress. "Hey, Elaine, can I get a coffee?"

She grinned at him. "Sure thing, Paul. Be right there."

Paul slid into the booth opposite his boss. "Not like you to take a break. You okay?"

"I'm fine." Nick folded up the paper and dropped it on the bench beside him. "I'm just tired. I was up most of last night and up early this morning. I think I had about four hours' sleep."

"You're gettin' kinda old for that, buddy."

Elaine brought a mug and the coffee pot. She poured for Paul. "You want more, Chief?"

He slid the cup toward her. "Yes, please."

She poured him a refill and dropped a spoon on the table for Paul. "You boys want anything else?"

Nick slashed the air over the table with his hand. "No, I'm good."

"Nothing for me, Elaine," Paul said.

"Give me a holler if you change your mind." She walked off, stopping two tables down to freshen the coffee cups of two elderly men.

Nick scrubbed his face with his hands, then put

more sugar and creamer in his coffee. "I want you to put a man on protection detail," he told Paul as he stirred his coffee.

"Let me guess, on Jean Hays?" Paul put his spoon down and sipped his coffee.

Nick eyed him with bloodshot eyes.

Paul laughed. "No, I'm not accusing you of anything but I read the morning reports. Her tires were slashed day before yesterday and last night she was attacked. Nothing was missing so it wasn't a robbery. Someone is out to get her."

"That's the way I read it." Nick picked up his mug. "If she's driving around, have a cruiser follow her. She's still in the rental."

Paul nodded. "Will do. You think you might catch whoever it is in the act?"

"I hope so. I've had more crime this week than in the last six months." Nick watched the two old guys get up and leave.

"What do you think of her now?"

Nick brought his eyes back to Paul. "She's okay. Not the stuck-up Easterner I thought she'd be. I tried to get her to stay home this morning but she wouldn't have it. She's got a strong sense of commitment."

A smile spread across Paul's face. "You like her."

Nick snorted. "Hardly. But I admire her grit. She's back at the fairgrounds, some light blue scarf wrapped around her head to hide the bandages. She must have a hell of a headache but there she is, taking care of business." He finished off his coffee. "I've got to run out to Rancho Verde. Get someone on Vera MacIlroy. Seems there was an argument between her and Ina over quilts."

Paul nearly snorted his coffee. "Quilts?"

Nick shrugged. "It's not like I have a lot of leads here." He drained his cup. "Ina was a champion quilter or some such. Maybe it's something." The men got out of the booth and walked to the register.

"Sure thing, boss. Get someone on Vera MacIlroy. I'll call one of the patrols to tail Ms. Hays. If there's any trouble, I'll let you know."

CHAPTER THIRTY

As Jean walked to the Exhibits building, she could feel the sun beating down. It intensified her existing headache. It was almost noon and the sound of the carnival with the rides clanking, the music blasting and the kids screaming made her headache worse. The smell of popcorn and cotton candy filled the air. The sweet smell, almost burnt, turned Jean's stomach. She quickened her pace.

Inside the Exhibits building it was quieter. People were walking slowly along the displays, pointing out exceptional pieces of work or cheering when they recognized their own or a friend's name. The carnival music subsided to a tolerable level. She grabbed a bottle of water from the cooler.

Karen came up behind her. "What are you doing here? Shouldn't you be home resting?" She gave Jean a hug.

"There's no way I could stay home the first day of the fair. Don't be silly."

Karen walked her over to the Homemaking Arts

area and sat Jean down. "What did the doctor say? Do you have a concussion? Should you be driving?"

Jean laughed as she unscrewed the cap to the bottle of water. "Whoa there, one question at a time." She took a drink and recapped the bottle.

Karen grabbed a second chair and sat beside her friend. "Spill it. Tell me every detail."

"I've got a gash on my head where I was hit. You saw that in the hospital when you picked up the keys. The doctor says there's no concussion. I can drive but my rental car was here so Chief White gave me a ride over."

"Chief White? He played taxi for you?" Both eyebrows raised.

"He stopped by my house after I got home to try and convince me not to come here today."

"He was right." Karen pointed her finger at her friend. "You should be home resting."

"No, I should not. I should be here, especially since Arris is out." Jean waited as a family passed by them, the youngest boy dropping popcorn in a trail behind him. "Anyway, I was going to call a cab, but he offered to bring me over."

"Well!" Karen said. "I think he's sweet on you."

"I don't think so. It's more likely that he thinks I'm a pain in his backside. I've been involved in three separate incidents this week. I can't imagine that his statistics are going to look good when the town wants to review his performance."

Karen shrugged. "Maybe, maybe not. Did he say anything about who might have attacked you?"

"Nope. There were no fingerprints on the car. None of my stuff was stolen. No clues at all."

Karen leaned back in her chair; disappointment

covered her face. "That sucks." Her frown reflected concern. "So they don't know who hit you or why?"

Jean shook her head as she uncapped the bottle and took another drink. Now that she was out of the sun and the noise, her head felt better.

"So, whoever slashed your tires and attacked you can do it again?" Karen's voice rose. An elderly couple turned to stare. She waved at them and got back to Jean. "What's he doing about it?"

"I have no idea. I told him about Josh Marlow. As far as I can tell he hasn't questioned the man at all. They have questioned Arris, though. Twice." Just thinking about it annoyed her. It was as though the man was totally ignoring her suggestions.

"Maybe they're questioning a lot of people, Ina's family, friends, other people." Karen sat back in her chair again. "He might have a lead or two and not tell you."

"True. He came in to question me last night. He was quite emphatic that I keep my nose out of his business." Her sarcastic tone of voice let Karen know what she thought of that. "Anyway, here I am, four hours late, but here. Thanks for getting more water and ice, by the way."

"No biggie. I get water out of that cooler myself. Glad to help." Karen fussed with her tote bag, picking it up and putting it back down. "I may have something."

Jean pressed the cold water to her temples, hoping to help the headache. "What?"

"Well, I had dinner at home last night before I came back. Peggy and Tyler were there. I just had a feeling, a couple of times, about Tyler."

"Peggy's boyfriend, right? We haven't met."

"Right. Anyway, he was watching me when I left the kitchen. We'd just been talking about our visit to Marlow and your slashed tires. Maybe Tyler knows something."

Jean blinked. The headache made it hard to think. "Did he know Ina? Does he seem like the kind of guy to kill someone?"

"I have no idea." Karen sighed. "It's just more questions that we don't have answers for."

"Don't feel bad. I told Nick about Vera MacIlroy. He looked at me like I was nuts and to be honest, I felt like a nut."

"You had to tell him." Karen dug the building key out of her shorts pocket. "Here's your key back."

"Thanks." Jean pulled her key ring out of her pocket and put the key back on it. "I appreciate the help."

"We'll all give you a hand. The others told me to tell you that. Don't try to do everything alone."

A grin spread across Jean's face. "Thanks. That's so nice of everyone."

Karen put her arm around Jean and gave her a hug. "That's what friends do, sweetie. That's what friends do."

CHAPTER THIRTY-ONE

It was one in the afternoon when Nick drove his police SUV down the driveway of the K Bar Seven ranch. He pulled up in front of the bunkhouse trailer and rapped on the door. No answer. *They're out working. Maybe the barn.* He got in the truck and drove to the nearest barn. There were no work noises nor sounds of life. Nick passed by a chicken coop, the chicken-wire-fenced yard must have held about fifty chickens. The ranchers know what they're eating this winter, he thought as he drove by. Where else could these guys be?

After a stop at the ranch house for directions, he drove out on the ranch road to a pasture next to the river. He found four ranch hands stringing fence wire. He got out of the car. The heat hit him hard after the car's air-conditioning. It must have been ten or fifteen degrees warmer than in Greyson. The men watched him, all except one. "Josh Marlow!" Nick called out.

The other three went back to work. The fourth man turned around. "Yeah. Who's askin'?"

Nick put his Stetson on—the sun was brutal—and walked over to the group. "Greyson Police Chief, Nick White. I'd like to ask you a few questions."

Josh glanced at the other ranch hands. They didn't meet his eyes. "Yeah, whatever." He jerked off his leather work gloves and slapped the dirt out of them against his blue-jeaned leg.

Josh's "whatever" set Nick's teeth on edge. He hated that phrase. "Let's step over here, sir." Nick pointed to the other side of the car.

"Sure, why not." Josh sauntered over to the far side of the car, the Chief following.

Nick adjusted his equipment belt and checked that his weapon was strapped down. He didn't like Marlow's attitude and wouldn't put it past the man to do something stupid. Nick stopped three feet away from the ranch hand. "Where were you between ten and midnight last night?"

Josh turned his head and spit in the dirt. "Right here."

"Can anyone corroborate that?"

Marlow jerked his head at the other hands. "They can. We all live in the same crappy trailer the owners call a bunkhouse." He stuck his hands in his front pockets. "What's this about?"

"How about day before yesterday, between midnight and six am? Where were you?"

The man drew a big breath. "Same place, right here. We get up early, I was in bed."

Nick didn't like the sullen look he was getting. "Sleeping? All of you?"

Josh smirked at the Chief. "Yeah."

"So you could have left for a while, come back, and no one would have been the wiser?"

"What are you gettin' at, Chief?" He took a step forward, anger straining his voice.

Nick tapped his weapon and the man backed up. "I've got a couple of attacks on people in town. I'm just trying to sort out the facts."

Josh's eyes shifted to his buddies, who were pretending to string wire. They hadn't moved a step since Nick arrived. "I didn't attack anybody."

Nick looked pointedly at the ranch hands. They worked faster. "Hmm. You have a car?"

"Yeah," Josh replied in a sullen tone. "So what?"

"Just sayin'. It's not that far to Greyson and back. If a man has his own ride."

"Look." Josh started to take a step and Nick could see him think better of it and step back. "I didn't attack anybody. I was right here."

"So you say. If I separate you all and ask them," he jerked his chin at the trio on the fence, "what would they say?"

Josh's gaze strayed to the other men. "Just what I said. I was here."

Nick nodded. "I heard that you and Ina Grange were an item for a while last year."

"So?" The ranch hand pulled his hands out of his pockets and crossed his arms. "What of it?

"I heard she broke up with you. Did that make you mad?"

"She did not break up with me! I dumped her. The cow was too old."

Nick whipped his sunglasses off as he took a step forward, and he pointed them at Marlow's chest. "You will keep a civil tongue in your head. You hear me?"

Josh scuffed his boots in the dust and looked at his

feet. "Yeah."

"When's the last time you saw Ina?"

"I don't know. It's been months." Josh's voice came out whiney.

"Take a guess," Nick prodded.

Marlow shook his head. "A year since we broke up. I'd see her and that ass Arris dancin' sometimes."

"I warned you about your mouth."

The ranch hand scowled at the dirt. "That's it. Just saw them out once in awhile, when I come to town on my day off."

Nick didn't have a good feeling."You sure?"

Josh jerked his head up. "Yeah. I'm sure." Defiance had crept back in his voice.

Something was off but Nick couldn't put a finger on it. "Yep. You can go."

Josh nodded and walked back to his work.

Nick watched as Marlow rejoined the group. None of them said a word. He walked around the SUV and got in, started the engine and made a circle to turn around. As he slowly drove off he could see one of the ranch hands yelling at Josh. Josh reached out and punched him in the arm. "Hmm," Nick hummed aloud. "Not best buds after all." He tucked that information away in the back of his mind and drove back to Greyson.

CHAPTER THIRTY-TWO

Jean was sitting in a quiet corner of the Exhibits building, dozing. After the attack, the sleepless night in the hospital, and the excitement of the first day of the fair, she was exhausted. She'd noticed that the Gems and Minerals area had an unused corner where there was little traffic. She told Karen, then John Gonzales, that she was going to catnap there and to call her if they needed her.

It felt odd to her that she felt safe enough to sleep in the middle of the fair. It wasn't like her at all. She could admit that she was a bit of a control freak. Sleeping in a public place seemed the height of folly but she felt so secure. Odd noises intruded, but they were infrequent. The music of the carnival rides had melted into the background. The chit-chat between John and fairgoers about odd bits of stone was soothing. The sound of the building exhaust fan just over her head provided a kind of white noise. She sank in and out of sleep as though she were drifting on a warm ocean.

Her phone woke her. She started upright and yanked the phone out of her pocket. She stared bleary-eyed at the screen. It was four twenty pm. "Yeah."

"Jean? It's Jason Lerner. Over in Livestock?"

She rubbed the sleep from her eyes and yawned to get some oxygen into her brain. Despite the fans, it was hot in Exhibits. "What's up, Jason?"

"It's a mess over here. The 4-H and FFA kids are washing their animals for show tonight and the drains are backed up and the water out of the hoses has turned into a trickle. The kids are frantic."

Jean sucked in a deep breath, trying to get her brain to work. "Let me see if I can get someone out here. I'll call you back."

"Hurry, Jean. The first round of the livestock show starts at six. The kids need their animals groomed."

She stood up and arched her back. Her headache roared to the front of her head. "I'll get right on it, Jason." She clicked off and hurried to the middle of the building where her notebook was tucked under an exhibit stand.

Karen hurried over to her as she was flipping through the notebook. "What's going on?"

"The livestock wash racks are clogged and the water isn't flowing from the hoses. I need to find the plumber's number."

Jean flipped more pages. "Ha, here it is, Bob Martin." She dialed the number and gave Karen a wink. "Hi, Bob Martin please."

A young female voice answered. "Bob is out on a call right now. May I take a message?"

Jean drew a deep breath. She needed help right now. "Uh, this is Jean Hays at the fair. I have a clogged drain at the livestock wash rack and water isn't flowing to the hoses. Can I claim this as an emergency? The kids are depending on this. Their first show is at six tonight."

"I'll see what I can do, Ms. Hays. Our nephew has a steer in the fair this year. We'll do what we can."

"Thank you. I appreciate it." Jean sighed with relief. "Can you have him call me when he's on his way?"

"I'll do that, Ms. Hays."

Jean clicked off and turned to Karen. "The woman said she'd call him. They have a nephew with a cow in the fair."

"That's Bob's wife. They're good people. He did a great job with the fair last year. Hang in there."

"Okay." She tried to force her eyes open. "I'll walk over to Livestock and see what's going on. I could use the fresh air."

Karen's eyebrow rose. "You sure about that? It's at least ninety out there this afternoon."

"I'm sure." Jean sucked in a deep breath. "I need to move. And anyway, I haven't seen the barns yet. How can I miss the livestock part of the fair?"

"You know best what you can do. If you feel faint, though, don't tough it out. Sit down, even if it's in the dirt."

Jean saluted with a grin. "Yes, ma'am. I'll be careful."

Karen waved her away and went back to her department. Jean adjusted her headscarf and left the building. As soon as she stepped into the light, the sun hit her like a brick. She'd still expected September to be cooler than this. There was a walkway from the middle door to the end of the building going toward the livestock area. She followed that to the end of the building, then stepped off of the end of the walk and toward the north-west side of the fairgrounds. That's where the two livestock barns were. One barn held large livestock - cows, pigs and horses. The second barn held small livestock - sheep, goats, poultry, and a few guinea pigs, rabbits and other fowl such as duck, turkeys and geese.

She found Jason in the pig area, next to an excellent example of a Meishan pig according to the sign over the stall. It was drawing a lot of attention. "Hi Jason," she said when a break in his conversation opened.

He took a good look at her scarf. "I heard you were attacked. Are you all right?"

She shrugged. "I've had a headache all day, but I'm fine." She pointed her chin at the pig. "I've never seen that breed before."

"It's a beauty, all right. Andy Morrison's boy, Mike, raised him. It's a new breed for us and drawing a bit of attention. I think he'll do well at the auction."

"I called the plumber, Bob Martin. I understand he has a nephew with an animal here. He'll be along as fast as he can."

Jason frowned. "If the rest of the kids can't get their animals washed and groomed, it won't be fair for them to compete. I may have to postpone the event."

"He's coming as fast as he can, Jason. Is there somewhere else the animals can be washed?"

The VP of Livestock took off his cowboy hat and scratched his head through his gray hair. "I don't know. The Health Department is pretty picky, animal waste and all."

Jean nodded. She didn't want to interrupt his train

of thought.

"There's got to be good drainage. The ground is just clay here. The water runs off, it doesn't sink in." He reset his hat. "I don't know. Maybe we could get the fire department tanker in and wash the animals over by the wash. We'd have to make sure the water pressure wasn't too high."

"Who do I have to call, Jason?" Her cell phone rang. "Hello?"

"It's Bob Martin. You've got a problem in Livestock?"

"Yes, Bob. You know where the livestock wash rack is?"

"Yep. I'll be there shortly."

"Sure. I'll be here with Jason Lerner. See you here in a few." She clicked off.

Jason's face was all interest.

"Bob's on his way. Can you hold off on the fire department till Bob gets here?"

"Sure. I think we can wait. Let me show you around till he does."

Jason took her around the barn, explaining the finer points of cattle judging and introducing her to the kids who'd raised the animals. They had just finished their rounds of the large livestock barn when Bob found them.

"Hello, Bob." Jean shook his hand. "We appreciate you coming out."

"Glad to help." He shook hands with Jason. "Hey there, Jason. Can you show me the problem?"

Jean let the two men walk off to survey the damage. She went over to the small livestock barn. There she felt more at ease. The large livestock were good. She'd taken some very good pictures of kids with their Brown Swiss and Holsteins in upstate New York but here she found more beef steers than dairy cattle. Black Angus and Longhorns were predominant. The small livestock were cuter, though. Goats and sheep came right up to the fences and looked her in the eye. The sheep, at least most of them, were washed, sheared and covered with body-fitting covers to keep them clean. The kids with the animals not yet groomed looked sick with worry. Jean felt bad and hoped Bob could do something quickly.

Her phone rang. "Yes?"

"Bob, here. I've found the problem. It will take me about half an hour to clear the clogged drain. The water pressure in the hoses is still being looked at."

"Thanks Bob. I appreciate it."

While she was thinking about whether to make an announcement, Jason strode into the barn. "Listen up," he yelled. All of the exhibitors turned toward him. He gave them the information Bob had just given her. The kids all cheered. Jean felt better.

Jason walked over. "Some good news, at least."

"Yeah. They can wash the animals with low water pressure. They can't do anything if the drains are clogged."

Jason grinned at her. "You're pretty quick."

She grinned back. "I try. I'm going back to Exhibits. Keep me updated, will you?"

He tipped his hat. "I'll do that."

"Oh, Bob will give you a bill. Just have one of the kids run it over to me."

"Sure." He paused. "Thanks for steppin' up." He looked around the barn, satisfaction on his face. "We appreciate it."

"I'm just a volunteer, same as you. But I take your

meaning. You're welcome."

He nodded and left the building. Jean smiled to herself. *Nice people. I'm glad I moved here.*

CHAPTER THIRTY-THREE

Jean left the livestock barns and headed back to the Exhibits building. She could feel the sweat trickle down her back and the glare from the overhead sun still made her head ache. The gash on her head itched as sweat formed on her scalp. She resisted the urge to start scratching at it.

She was halfway back to the Exhibits tent when she noticed a police officer in full khaki uniform, white police Stetson on his head, walking behind her about fifty feet back. She stopped and knelt down to pretend-tie her shoe. The officer stopped too, staring nonchalantly in the direction of the bandstand where there was a watermelon-eating contest in progress. She could feel her stress levels rise. A peek to her right and left showed only normal fairgoers walking past in both directions. The officer checked his watch and readjusted his hat.

She had spent time in hostile countries building computer installations for the Air Force. Jean had been trained to identify people who may be following her. She re-tied her sneaker and stood up. The officer bent over to slap dust from the bottom of his pant legs. Jean swore under her breath. She was being followed. *Damn it, Chief. I don't need a babysitter!* She strode off, surprising the young officer who'd been assigned to follow her. A quick glance showed him unclipping the radio from his left shoulder and making a call.

Jean charged into the Exhibits building. She found Karen sitting in a folding chair in a corner of her area, a cross-stitch hoop in her hand and a needle with sky blue thread being poked through the cloth from top to bottom. She slammed into the chair next to Karen.

Karen's eyebrow went up. "Bad day?"

"I'm being followed," Jean blurted out. "Unbelievable." She crossed her arms over her chest and scowled.

Karen's needlepoint dropped into her lap. "Is it your attacker?" She turned full-on to her friend.

So angry that she wasn't hearing her friend, Jean said, "What?"

"Is it your attacker? The person who bashed your head in?" Exasperation was clear in Karen's voice.

"No!" Jean blinked and shook her head. Understanding flooded her mind. "No, it's the cops. Chief White is having a uniformed officer follow me around."

Karen reached out and slapped her friend on the arm. "Don't ever do that to me again!" She glared at Jean. "You scared the tar out of me."

"I'm so sorry." Jean reached out to Karen. "I was so angry about being babysat I didn't think about how the words came out. I apologize."

"You'd better be sorry. Scared me to death." She

picked up her cross-stitch. "And I think the Chief is right. You've been attacked, one way or another, twice in two days. You need protection."

Jean bristled. "I don't need protection. I'm perfectly capable of handling myself."

Karen eyed the scarf over Jean's head.

"Well, most of the time." Jean slammed herself back into the chair. "I've had self-defense classes."

"And how's that working out for you?" Karen asked, more than a tinge of snark in her voice.

"Shut up."

Karen laughed and kept on with her cross-stitching project.

"Fine. I was caught off guard once."

The two watched a pair of elderly women examine the quilt that had won the Best of Show ribbon.

"I see Vera MacIlroy won Best of Show."

Karen snorted. "Yep. I saw her over there earlier with her friends, gloating, her friends cooing and oohing. And Ina in the morgue. I wanted to go over there and smack them."

"Well, I suppose she's waited a long time for a win. Too bad it had to be because someone killed Ina. I wish I knew if the Chief was tracking down the Vera lead, silly or not." She fussed with her scarf. It was too loose.

"Their lives are so stable," Jean commented as the two elderly women walked away.

"They seem stable to us, at this moment." Karen tied off the color she was using and selected a light orange thread already on a needle. "We don't know what their lives are like. They could be a day away from an empty cupboard and could have spent their last dollar to come here and see some crafts and share a bit of companionship with their best friend. We just don't know."

Jean frowned. "Aren't you all Miss Optimism today."

"It's the truth and you know it. Just like you know you're safer with an officer following you around."

Jean looked up at the middle door. The officer was standing just inside, out of the sun. She could tell from where he was standing that he could see where she was. The thought galled. She was a grown woman. She didn't need a babysitter. Then the memory of the feeling in her stomach when she was attacked in the parking lot came flooding back. She thought she was going to be sick. "Maybe."

She got up and walked over to the door and reached under the exhibit stand where she kept their cooler of water. Jean pulled two bottles of water out of the cooler. In three steps she was next to the officer. "I saw you following me."

The young man nodded. "Yes, ma'am."

"You were assigned to follow me?"

His eyes darted around the room. His hands rested on his equipment belt. "Yes, ma'am."

Jean handed him a bottle of water. "You'll need to stay hydrated. There's no AC in this building."

The young officer touched the brim of his hat in salute. "Thank you, ma'am." He twisted the top off of the bottle and drank half of it down.

"There's more in the cooler under the display. Help yourself."

"Thank you, ma'am."

Jean walked back to the chair next to Karen and sat down. She uncapped her bottle of water and took a sip. She wiped the cold water from the outside of the bottle on her temples. It helped a little bit with the headache.

"See?" Karen grinned. "That wasn't so hard."

Jean recapped the bottle. "Mind your own business."

Karen just laughed.

CHAPTER THIRTY-FOUR

It was after seven at night. Nick had checked with the lab and received dismal news. Nothing they'd checked so far from the storage container had unusual prints on them. It was all people who should have been handling the boxes, totes, tools and the other things in the container. He made a note to himself to check whether Josh Marlow had ever volunteered for any events at the fairground and turned out his desk lamp.

He locked his office door. His secretary had left at five so he locked the outer office door too. Nick waved to the on-duty officer who was stationed at the reception window. They had to have an officer on duty in the station so she was put there. The duty rotated among the whole staff so no one could complain they were stuck on a desk. Nick couldn't see paying a civilian to sit there napping all night. All station calls were routed to that position. "I'm going over to the fairgrounds with Paul. My cell is on."

"Gotcha, Chief. Have fun." The officer waved.

Outside Nick got into his SUV and headed to the

fairgrounds. He parked and walked to the large livestock barn where his niece, Morgan, had her Black Angus steer. She was in the stall, fastening her blue ribbon to the brag board at the back. "Hey there, punkin' head! Looks like you did all right in the first round."

The girl squealed and ran over to her uncle and gave him a hug through the bars of the stall gate. "Hi Uncle Nick. I thought I wasn't going to be able to show but the water got fixed and I groomed Rusty just in time to make my turn."

He nodded, confused. His sister, Tracy Marks, gave him a hug. "The drain clogged and the water slowed to a trickle. It was fixed by five. The first round showing lineup was juggled to give the kids who hadn't groomed their animals later start times."

"Ah." He reached out and pretend-pinched his niece's nose. "You did just fine then. When's the next showing?"

"Tomorrow," the girl chirped. She gave her steer a hug. "Me and Rusty are going to get the Grand Champion ribbon, aren't we boy?" She stroked the animal's face between its eyes.

Nick raised his eyebrows at his sister and they walked off together around the barn. The place was a hive of activity. Final food and water for the day was being given to each animal by its owners. Kids were displaying their ribbons on back boards. Families were handing out sacks of fast food for dinner. Spare stalls were set up as little family enclaves where they could hang out, visit with other ranch families and keep an eye on the animals.

Fair goers wandered through the barn as well, stopping to admire a healthy-looking steer or pig.

Tracy greeted many of the families and Nick did as well. His position was elected, and while he was mainly there to see his sister and her family, it didn't hurt to remind the voters that he was one of them.

Paul caught up to him at the last stall in the barn. "Hey, there. I see you started without me." He gave Tracy a hug. "Where's that old man of yours?"

"He's over in the small livestock barn with Daniel. They're feeding the sheep and goats."

"Tell him hi for me. I fully intend to beat him next Saturday on the golf course."

"I'll tell him," she laughed. The two men, high school friends and rivals, had an ongoing challenge every other week on the golf course.

Nick gave his sister another hug. "I'm going to take a stroll around the fair. I'll try and get over here tomorrow for the next judging rounds. Call me with the times."

"I'll do that. Dan and Morgan would be thrilled if you could watch."

Paul tipped his police Stetson. "Have a good night, Tracy."

She waved, then headed back to Rusty's stall.

They ran into Jason Lerner outside the barn. "Hey there, Jason," Nick said. The men all shook hands. "Heard you had some trouble this afternoon." The music of the carnival drifted over them.

"We did. The livestock wash rack drain clogged up. I've been telling the maintenance people about that drain for a year. Well, they had to do something about it, finally, today. That new woman, Jean? She got a plumber right on it."

Paul winked at Nick, who glared back. "I'm glad it was resolved. My niece, you know Morgan, was one of the ones affected."

"Oh, yeah, good kid. She was a trooper. And she did really well at the first round showing. That Rusty is a fine steer. I may have to bid on him myself."

A grin spread across Nick's face. He appreciated it when his niece and nephew received compliments. "Thanks, Jason. I'll tell them you said so."

The three men said good night and moved on. Paul looked at Nick out of the corner of his eye. "Hey, let's go look at the exhibits. My aunt has some pickles in the Canned-Goods department."

Nick shot him a look. "How about we go over to the midway and get something to eat. I missed lunch."

Paul laughed. "Fair enough. Let's get the barbeque. I could use a pulled pork."

The two strolled, taking in the flow of people buying food. Nick stopped to glare at a foursome of teen boys, rough-housing next to a full trash can. The boys caught the look and moved on, still punching at each other. The men walked on.

"Hard to believe we were that silly," Paul said.

"We were never that silly. We both had a full load at school, ranch chores to do and after-school jobs to go to."

Paul laughed. "Oh yeah? What about the time you, me, Lyle Andrews and Jerry Cole took three days off to run up to President Lake the summer after we graduated? I distinctly remember—"

Nick held up a hand. "I was there. I remember. We were lucky none of us got killed that weekend." He drew in a deep breath and became quiet. After a few steps he said, "Shame about Lyle. He would have been a good man."

Paul grew somber as well. "Damn shame. That elk

went right through the windshield. Freak accident."

"Yeah. He was the smartest of us. He would have made a fine doctor one day."

"Yep."

The men reached the barbeque trailer and each ordered a pulled pork. They continued walking around the grounds toward the Exhibits building after they each had one in hand. "How's Ms. Hays?" Paul asked around a mouthful of pork.

"I haven't seen her since I brought her over here this morning,"

"You drove her over here?"

Nick swallowed. "Yeah. I tried to talk her out of coming. She insisted on coming here as soon as she got out of the hospital. I know her head had to be splitting."

Paul grinned. "I saw in the morning report you did the interview in the hospital."

Nick's voice went hard. "She was assaulted. How the hell often does that happen in Greyson? And not a thing stolen, so it wasn't a druggie."

"You think someone has it out for her?" Paul stopped grinning. "You don't think they'd murder her, do you?"

"Well they had their chance. She was unconscious." Nick ate the last bite of his sandwich and threw the paper wrapper in the trash. He pulled a napkin from his pocket and wiped his hands and threw that in too, then walked on. "I've got my eye on Josh Marlow."

Paul had to think a moment. "Ranch hand down in Rancho Verde?"

"That's the guy. He's got a history of bar fights and drunk and disorderly."

"Big jump from that to murder, Nick."

"Maybe so, but something about the guy sets my teeth on edge. I'm going to keep an eye on him while I check out other leads."

"Fair enough. What do you want me to do?"

"Check out the other ranch hands. Marlow bunks with three or four other guys. I'm going to look into Ina's family. She had a gambling problem. That might make someone angry. Maybe even the casino, though I think that's a long shot. Jimmy Crowfoot assured me they use attorneys for debt collection. I need you to look into the companies the casino is using to collect gambling debts. See if there's any funny business going on there. Reports of people getting roughed up, stuff like that. And check with the track down in Phoenix. Maybe they had some hinky collection agency do something, too."

"What a mess," Paul said.

"Tell me about it." Nick hoped he was covering all the bases.

CHAPTER THIRTY-FIVE

When she got out of the rental car the next morning, Jean adjusted the gray scarf she'd wrapped around her head. *This is what I get for taking a sleep aid. Late!* The very fact she was two hours late made her crazy. She was never late, for anything. But between the head injury, the bad dreams and the minor sleep aid, she'd overslept. *'Minor sleep aid' my ass.* She silently cursed the doctor who had told her it was very mild. She hurried through the back gate, where the exhibitors and fair workers entered, and rushed to the Exhibitor Building. It was already nine in the morning. An hour after the fair opened. Jean was sick with embarrassment.

She skidded to a halt outside the west end of the Exhibitor Building. It was open. A family of five exited the door, the mother nodding to her as they passed. She took a deep breath and walked into the building.

Several families and couples were inside, pausing at the school exhibits, the fine arts and the photography display. Jean smiled and nodded. When she paused in the photography area an elderly woman, Jean guessed about seventy-five, asked, "How do I enter an exhibit?"

Jean led her to the table the photography Superintendent had set up with the help of the local photography club. She introduced the woman to the club member on duty there and drifted away. The woman waved when Jean left.

Well, good to know I'm not a complete waste of space. She wound her way around exhibits and fairgoers. She still had a headache. Jean adjusted the scarf again. It was falling over her left eye.

When she arrived at the middle of the building, Karen was waiting for her. "You got some rest!"

Jean shook her head. "Not so much. Horrible dreams, sleeping drugs, it was all bad. Thank you for opening."

Karen gave her a hug. "Not a problem. You still have a headache, don't you?"

An eyeroll gave Karen all the ammunition she needed. "Why are you here? Just go home. Sleep. Relax. We can do this."

"I feel guilty." Jean sank onto the chair next to the one Karen usually used. "I signed on to volunteer, not lay about my house at the most important time."

"Oh, for gosh sakes! You were bashed in the head. You *get* to lay about!"

Jean eyed her friend. "You're trying to take over, you are? Power mad, you are!" Jean's voice rasped in her best Yoda impersonation.

Karen slapped her on the arm. "That was awful. Does that work for you?"

Jean laughed, until she had to press her hand to

her scalp wound. "Ow. That hurts. Don't make me laugh."

Karen glared at her in response. "Really. Why are you here?"

A nod in the direction of the middle door was her answer. "He was back with me at eight. There was a car outside on the curb in front of my house at nine pm. Another car was there at six. Mr. Police Protector was standing at the gate to follow me in when I got here. I'm starting to feel like bait."

"The Chief and his deputy were through here last night just after you left."

Jean rolled her eyes. "Don't tell me. They wanted to question me?"

Karen snorted a laugh. "No. They wanted to see Paul's aunt's pickles in Canning."

A blush crept up Jean's face. "Excuse me!" She shifted on the chair. "That's all?"

"Yep." Karen walked over to a display table and readjusted a crooked entry. "They were pretty casual about it, but I noticed the Chief looking around the building."

"He's a cop. He's trained to look around and notice things." Jean crossed her arms over her chest. *Was he looking around for me?* She seriously doubted it but was intrigued nonetheless.

Karen's right eyebrow arched. "Of course."

"I'm going to get something to eat." Jean stood up, sliding the chair back. "You want something?"

"Yeah, an order of those curly fries drenched in cheese."

Jean's eyes went wide. "Seriously?"

"Oh, yeah. I wait all year for those suckers. Can I give you some money?" Karen headed for her purse.

"Nonsense. I'm buying." Jean waved her off. "But I can't believe Ms. Healthy Food is asking for that."

Karen stared at her wide-eyed. "It's fair food. Once a year! Get me my fries!" She pointed imperiously.

Jean bowed. "To hear is to obey. Cheesy curly fries on their way."

After grabbing her wallet, Jean strolled out of the building and toward the midway. The craft fair was in the space between her building and the midway. Jean walked from booth to booth looking at the jewelry, hand-made soaps, end-of-season vegetables, knitted goods, hand-crafted dolls and rugs and wood-worked wares. She stopped to talk to most of the vendors, asking them about their sales and fair experience so far. At the wood-working booth she bought an exotic wood pen for her son. It would make a good Christmas gift.

She was constantly aware of the young officer behind her. Today he was in civilian clothing. She had to admit he blended in better that way, though it still bugged her that he had to follow her at all.

As Jean approached the midway, she spied Analise's gourmet sandwich truck. It was still a little early for the lunch crowd but Jean saw a young man—dark hair, dark complexion, wearing cowboy boots, jeans and a western-style shirt—standing at the window, arguing with Analise. She was too far away to hear what was being said. He waved his arm, and Analise pointed at him, her face the picture of anger. *What's going on there?* Jean shifted her bag from the wood-worker from one hand to the other. She closed on the food truck, doing her best to stay out of sight of the window.

"You'll be sorry." The young man flung his hands up and stormed off, away from Jean. *Too bad I couldn't hear the whole conversation.* She checked her escort. He was looking at the display of children's toys three stalls behind Jean. *Of course he has small children. And now that he's following me, he isn't going to have time to bring his family to the fair.* Jean sighed as the cloak of guilt settled over her. Damn!

Jean drifted by the sandwich truck. Analise was on the phone inside, her back to the window.

"I don't care. Just take care of it," Jean overheard her say, but then Analise hung up. *Something isn't right here.* But Jean could hardly hang around the sandwich truck all day waiting for something else to happen, so she decided to move on. *I wouldn't buy a sandwich from that woman on a bet. I might just as well say, "Come poison me."* She walked down to the Knights of Columbus stand.

"A brat, please."

An older man took her money and handed her the tiny tray covered with a grill-toasted bun and a charred brat. He pointed out the mustard.

As she bit into the sausage through the crisp skin, the fat from the dog spurted out and splashed on the bun. *Not as good as the rindwurst in Germany, but it will do.* Jean eyed Analise's truck; she was taking a sandwich order. No more clues there for the time being.

CHAPTER THIRTY-SIX

Jean finished her brat as she stood beside the Knights of Columbus cart. They told her this year's fair was good for them. There were a lot of people attending this year. One old guy joked, "Nothing like a dead body to bring people in." Jean smiled while thinking there was nothing funny about a dead body falling on you. She thanked them for the brat, tossed her trash in the nearby can and walked on.

Moving along the midway, she stopped and introduced herself and asked each vendor how they were doing. As to be expected, some were doing better than others. She thanked each of them for coming to the fair and walked to the next vendor. It was nice to see families out, enjoying the event. Kids raced up and down the midway, balloons dancing in the air behind them. Teens walked by in pairs or packs, eating shaved ice or cotton candy or popcorn. Girls in pairs whispered to each other. Boys tended to push, shove, smack and otherwise annoy the others in their group. She remembered that from when her son was a teen. Boys just couldn't seem to hold still.

Halfway down the midway she noticed a commotion by one of the picnic tables. She hurried over. A middle-aged woman hovered over an elderly man as another woman fanned him with her napkin. Jean interrupted. "Is something wrong? I'm with the fair."

The woman fanning looked worried. The middle-aged woman said, "My dad is having problems with the heat."

Jean moved in. The man was pale, but not sweating. He panted as he sat on the picnic table bench and his eyes were beginning to roll back in his head. "How long has he been like this?"

"Just a minute. He said he didn't feel good and we sat down here."

Jean pulled off the scarf over her head, exposing the bandages. *Thank goodness I wore a cotton one today.* She glanced around. There was a bottle of water on the table. "Is that your water?"

The woman nodded. Jean grabbed it, soaked her scarf with the water and put the wet cloth on the man's head. She turned around. Her escort was a few steps away. "Officer, call an ambulance. I suspect this man is suffering from heat exhaustion, maybe worse." She saw him pull a cell phone from his pocket and turned back to the family. "I'm Jean. We're calling an ambulance."

The younger woman said, "I'm Mae, this is my mom Willa and my dad is Henry. I don't understand. Dad was drinking a lot of water."

Jean nodded. "That helps, of course, but in this case we need to bring his body temperature down and drinking water won't help. We need to cool him down. Head first, then neck, wrists and so on as best we can. Can you go over to the vendor there and get me three more bottles of water? As cold as they have them."

Mae nodded and hurried off.

"Willa, how are you? Are you too hot, too?"

The woman, in her late sixties as far as Jean could tell, shook her head. "No, I feel fine. Henry had a cold last week. I wondered if he felt well enough to come out today but he insisted." She wiped an unshed tear from her eye. "Bull-headed, always was."

Mae rushed back. "Here." She thrust the bottles at Jean.

Jean uncapped one and took the scarf from his head. The water she poured over it was ice cold. She put it back on his head. "Do you have a scarf, bandana, anything?"

Both women shook their heads. A voice from behind Jean broke in. "I have a bandana." She turned around. A young man in well-worn, dusty cowboy boots, dirty jeans and grubby western-style shirt pulled a bandana out of his shirt pocket. "Take it. I have a lot more."

Jean nodded her thanks and took the bandana. It was clean. She unfolded it and poured water over it, then wrapped it around Henry's neck. Two more people handed her a handkerchief and another bandana. She wet them and wrapped them around Henry's wrists. The officer moved closer to her. "Ambulance is on the way. It's about five minutes out."

"Thank you." She looked at him. "I don't know your name."

"Williams." He tipped his cowboy hat.

"Thank you, Officer Williams."

"Not a bother, Ms. Hays." He drifted to the back of the small crowd.

The next few minutes were spent rewetting the cloths to cool them off and getting Henry to drink some of the cold water. Officer Williams cleared a path through the crowd when the EMTs arrived with a stretcher. Jean stepped back and let the crew do their job. Willa went with the EMTs when they rolled the stretcher away. Mae shook Jean's hand. "Thank you for the help. I just didn't know what to do."

"I was glad to help. Do you need a ride to the hospital?"

"No." She sniffed, wiping at a few tears. "I'm going to drive over. I just wanted to take a second to say how grateful we are."

"You're welcome. I hope he recovers quickly."

"Me, too." Mae hurried away.

Jean took a breath. The crowd had melted away now that the drama was over. She caught a few passersby looking at her head. A flash of embarrassment washed over her, but then she shook it off. *I've got nothing to be embarrassed by. I have a wound, it's bandaged.* She stood up straight and held her head up. She continued her visit to each vendor. Four booths away a woman was selling hand-dyed silk scarves.

"I heard what you did," she said after they had introduced themselves. She pulled a sage green scarf from the rack. "Take this to cover the bandages."

"Oh, I can't do that." Jean raised her hands to refuse the gift. "That's too much."

"Nonsense," the vendor told her. "Come on in. I know a cute way to tie it."

Jean   hesitated.
"Come on." The woman waved her into the booth.
"It will go well with your blouse."

After another moment, Jean accepted. "Thank
you. You're too kind."

"One good deed deserves another, my mother
always told me." She stood behind Jean and put the
scarf around her head. Jean could feel the woman
wrapping and tying. "There. Take a look." She handed
Jean a mirror.

The scarf ends had been wrapped from back to
front and around again, and the knot in the back
looked like a little flower. "Oh, how cute!" She
fingered the knot. "That's very clever. Thank you."

The woman grinned. "I do my nieces' scarves up
for them all the time. It's fun to share."

Jean shook her hand. "You've been so wonderful.
I appreciate it."

The two women exchanged hugs and said
goodbye. They waved to each other as Jean left. As
she walked away she felt good and realized her
headache was gone. She also realized the tension was
gone, tension she hadn't realized she'd been carrying.
Trust, she thought to herself. *You didn't trust anyone
after the attack. Now you do.* It felt as though a huge
weight had been lifted. The day seemed brighter. She
stopped at an ice cream vendor and bought two
vanilla ice cream cones. After she paid, she turned
around and spotted her minder. Jean walked over to
him and handed him a cone.

"This is for you."

Surprise covered his face, then embarrassment as
he glanced around to see who might be watching.

"Go on, take it. It's a hot day and you've had to

follow me around for a day and a half already. Enjoy yourself a little. It's a fair."

He hesitated, then took the cone.

"I hope vanilla is okay."

"It's just fine. Thank you." He took a lick.

"It seems goodwill and kindness is just flowing through the midway today." Jean began her walk back to the Exhibits building. Officer Williams waited. "Oh, no. No more trailing behind me. Walk with me. Tell me about yourself and your family."

His eyes widened.

"I'm serious." Jean waved him to her side. "Let's get to know each other."

He moved up beside her and they walked off together. "What's your first name?" By the time they arrived at the building, she knew he was Tom, had a wife, Glenna, a six-year-old boy, Randy, and a three-year-old girl, Emma.

It wasn't until she got back to the building and looked at Karen that she remembered. "I forgot your fries." She slapped herself on the forehead with the palm of her hand. "I'll be right back." She spun around and hurried out of the building. "Sorry, Tom. I was supposed to get cheesy fries for Karen." Jean strode right along and went straight to the fries vendor. The booth was two up from Analise's sandwich truck. After she gave the man her order she watched the food truck while she waited. She saw another young man, this one blond, in sneakers, jeans and a t-shirt go up to the window. Analise motioned him around to the open door. Jean couldn't hear anything they said over the noise of the carnival music and the people walking by. She could, however, see Analise. The woman was obviously angry. She pointed at him over and over in short, sharp jabs. Whoever the young man was, he acted defensive, then got angry himself and pointed at her before storming off. Analise smacked the door frame of the truck and went back inside.

That was interesting. Jean looked around for Officer Williams. He was at the next booth getting a hot dog, so he hadn't seen the exchange. *I wonder what that argument was about?* Her musings were interrupted when the vendor said, "Here you go, Miss."

He handed her a heavy-duty paper plate covered with spiral-cut potato, deep fried and covered with melted cheese sauce. "Oh my."

He grinned. "It's my best seller."

"Thanks." She grinned back at him. "This is for a friend. I may have to come back later and get one for myself."

"See you then." He moved on to his next customer.

She picked up Officer Williams when she walked by. He was eating his hot dog. "Wow, that's a lot of fries."

"I know," she laughed. "I might get one myself, later."

He nodded. "I can see why."

They hurried. Jean didn't want Karen's food to get cold. On the way back she wondered about the two different young men arguing with Analise an hour apart. What would Analise be sorry for? And who was she telling to "just get it done?" Then the second young man. He seemed angry but not the same as the first man. She wished she could have heard that exchange. Analise seemed different with him than the first guy. It was a puzzle.

CHAPTER THIRTY-SEVEN

At seven Jean was hungry and there were two more hours before fair closing. She'd spent the day in the Exhibits building talking to the other volunteers. There had also been questions from visitors about the building, the exhibits and where things were on the fairgrounds. One interesting thing did happen, though. Two hours earlier Karen had called Jean over to the Homemaking Arts department.

"Jean, meet Vera MacIlroy." Jean had seen the woman and her friends yesterday, standing in front of her prize-winning quilt, but they hadn't spoken. Vera was in her sixties and was built like a farm hand. Her hair was drawn back into a severe gray bun and her pale blue eyes were surrounded by the wrinkles that came from working in the hot Arizona sun for decades.

"Nice to meet you, Ms. MacIlroy." Jean held out her hand and Vera shook it. It was a surprisingly firm grip for an old woman. "I saw you yesterday with your friends but I didn't have a chance to congratulate you on winning Best of Show."

"Call me Vera, I still think of Mrs. MacIlroy as my mother-in-law. And thank you. I've been trying to win that prize for years."

"Terrible thing about Ina." Jean studied the woman's reaction.

"It is." Vera shook her head. "I don't know what this county is coming to, murder right in the middle of town."

Jean tried another tack. "I understand Ina was your chief competitor. I heard you were quite upset at her last year."

"She was. And I was. I was so mad I spit on her quilt." Vera sighed. "I felt bad about it later. Not very Christian of me. I let my pride and my jealousy get the better of me. I apologized to her the next day. Then I went around and apologized to everyone who'd had to witness my childish behavior." Vera studied the floor at her feet, then lifted her head and straightened her spine. "I'm glad I apologized. I'd hate to have that on my conscience now that she's gone. She made beautiful quilts."

Jean could see genuine sadness on the woman's face. "I'm so sorry for your loss, Vera."

"Thank you." Vera sniffed and then smiled at Jean. "I hear you're new in town. How do you like Greyson?"

"I like it very much. There are a lot of nice people here."

"I'm glad. Feel free to stop by the Methodist Church on Sunday. Service is at ten." She grinned. "After the service is a potluck. I make a mean enchilada casserole."

"I appreciate the invitation, Vera. Enjoy the fair."

"I will. Nice to meet you."

"Nice to meet you, too." Jean and Karen watched as the woman rejoined her family.

"What do you think, Karen?" They saw Vera, her daughter and granddaughter wander off to the Photography department.

"I don't think she killed Ina."

"She's strong enough. She has a grip like a vise." Jean adjusted her scarf.

"But she was genuinely sad about Ina's death."

"And there were the apologies. That would be easy enough to check, so I don't think she was lying." Jean adjusted one of the afghans hanging on a display rack. "No, I'm with you. I don't think she did it."

#

Two hours later the traffic through the building was slow and Jean was a little bored. She adjusted her scarf, still tied the way the scarf vendor had left it. "I'm going to get something to eat," she called over to Karen.

Karen wandered over to where Jean was sitting. "I'm still full from the fries. Could you get me a lemonade? That will help cut all the grease I ate at lunchtime."

"I should think so," Jean laughed. She pulled her wallet out of the bag she had stashed away under the displays and stood up. "I won't be long."

"Take your time. It's only going to get slower." Karen went back to her chair where she had her needlepoint project and sat down.

Jean walked out into the cooling night air. It was still stuffy in the Exhibits building; much nicer outside. She strolled to the midway. The clientele had changed. During the day it was the elderly and families with young children. Now the people she passed were young adults, teenagers, and young couples, sometimes pushing a baby stroller. The carnival and midway were lit up like Times Square and the music from the carnival seemed even louder. How nice, she thought, that people are out having fun.

Memories surfaced of her and Dwight, taking Jimmy to a fair when the boy was about eight. They were just like the couple in front of her now - walking along hand in hand, child dancing along in front of them, pointing out every new and exciting thing, begging for every trinket or food item that caught his eye. She had to swallow the lump that began to form in her throat. That was a long time ago and far, far away. Jean took a breath and pushed the memory down. She was still too angry over the divorce to enjoy the memory of her son at the fair.

As she walked she evaluated the food selection. She'd had bratwurst for lunch so she wanted something else. The taco stand caught her eye. Tacos at the fair—a new thing for her, this being the southwest. In New York it had been fried dough with tomato sauce and a sprinkling of parmesan cheese. Here it was tacos and Navajo fry bread. The same as fried dough, but instead of tomato sauce, it was refried beans and cheese. She hurried over. "Two tacos, please. Beef and cheese."

While she waited she watched a group of teenaged girls go by, giggling and shrieking at their own conversation. A gaggle of teen boys followed along about twenty feet behind them. The girls turned occasionally to peek at the boys and peals of giggles sounded at each turn. Jean had to smile. Some things never changed.

#

Nick White got out of his car and flashed his badge to get through the gate. The woman in the booth waved him through. He made it a habit to come to the fair every day it was open, usually in the evening. That's when trouble came, if it happened at all. Generally it was some young guy who'd had too much to drink in the beer tent and gotten offended by something stupid, then started a fight. He hoped it stayed quiet this year. Most of his officers were interviewing people about Ina's murder. He didn't have a lot of officers left to cover a disturbance at the fair.

His stomach growled. *Yeah, yeah,* he told himself. *Stop skipping lunch. Fine, let's get something here.* He knew the guy who had the taco stand. The owner had a permanent setup in the parking lot of the local hardware store. Nick stopped by the stand at least once a week and tacos sounded good right now. He headed for the stand.

He saw Officer Williams before he saw Jean and stopped short. Nick spotted her at the stand counter, ordering. He waved his officer over.

"Hey, Chief." The young man stood at attention though he was in civilian clothing.

"Hey, Tom." Nick jerked his chin in Jean's direction. "How's it going?"

"Pretty dull, Chief, a lot of standing around doing nothing. There was some excitement this afternoon though."

Nick's interest perked up. "Oh?"

"Yeah. Some old guy had heat exhaustion. Ms. Hays stepped right in, pulled her scarf off of her head and got water and put it on the old guy's head. She took charge. Sent the daughter for cold water, got more handkerchiefs and bandanas from the crowd, had me call the ambulance. By the time the EMTs got here, she had cold compresses on all of the guy's pulse points and had calmed the wife and daughter down. It was a sight to see."

Nick cocked an eyebrow. "Good emergency first-aid skills."

"I thought so."

"Anything else?"

"Nope. She's buying dinner. I think I will, too."

"That's what I'm here for. I go to Jose's stand at least once a week." He clapped the young man on the shoulder. "Enjoy your dinner."

They stepped up to the counter and ordered. Tom drifted off to the left of the stand as Nick approached Jean.

"Hi there."

Jean turned. "Hi Nick. Checking up?"

"Yep. I come every night of the fair. Sometimes there's a little trouble over at the beer tent."

She nodded. "Anything yet on my attacker?"

"No, sorry." He stuck his hands in his pockets and watched the parade of people walking by.

"I saw something today. Three different things, matter of fact."

He drew a deep breath. "Go on."

Jean nodded toward Analise's food truck. "This morning I saw her talking with a young guy, mid-twenties, maybe, dark hair, an angry discussion. He told her she'd be sorry. Right after, I saw her make a call. She was upset and angry and told whoever she was talking to to take care of it. Then about an hour later I saw a different young man, blond, go to her window. She took him around to the truck door where I saw them have an argument. I couldn't hear, but there was a lot of finger-pointing and yelling. The blond guy stormed off. Analise didn't seem very happy."

She's still trying to be a detective, he grumbled to himself. "Doesn't sound like much. Do you know the guys?"

"No." She shook her head, sounding disappointed. She turned to face the Chief. "But I know an argument when I see it and they were both mad about something."

He did his best not to roll his eyes. "Could have been anything, Jean. She may owe the guy money, he may owe her money. Hell, knowing Analise, it could be a lover's quarrel."

"He couldn't be more than twenty-five!"

Nick's eyebrow went up. "It happens."

"I guess. But something is going on there, Nick. I just know it."

"All that police training?" As soon as he said it he wished he could pull the words back. He could see her face go from shock, to disbelief, then anger. He started to say he was sorry.

She held up a hand. "Not another word." Jean spun on her heel and left.

Tom hurried up. "What happened?"

"Nothing. I'll get your food. Follow her." Tom hurried off after the rapidly retreating Jean.

Put your foot in it that time, Nick, you fool. He watched Tom hurry after Jean. Behind him he heard Jose call out, "Nick, her order is ready."

"I'll take it to her, Jose." He turned to the counter. "Wrap it up, will you?"

"Sure, Nick."

"Mine and Tom's too."

Jose waved acknowledgement.

Nick stood and thought about what Jean had told him. *She has an eye, that's for sure. I should have said that, not some snarky response. I need to check out Analise some more. It's possible she is framing Arris. Damn. I just had to open my big mouth.*

Nick called Tom. "What else did Jean want?"

"She was getting lemonade for Karen."

Nick picked up the tacos and the lemonade—with an extra for Jean—and trudged over to the Exhibits building. He found Karen Carver in Homemaking Arts, the department empty, doing some sort of needlework.

"Hi." He handed her one of the lemonades. "Ms. Hays forgot her food."

Karen put down her work and took the lemonade. The plastic cup was wet with condensation and sticky to boot. "Thanks for the lemonade, Chief."

He swallowed. Hard. "Uh, Ms. Hays?"

Karen took a sip of the lemonade and screwed up her face. "Hoo, that's tart. Just the way I like it." She rolled the cup around, the ice stirring the drink with a soft rattle. "Jean gave me the keys to close up and left." Karen sat back in her chair and eyed the bags in his hands. "I guess she decided she wasn't hungry after all."

That made him feel worse. Now the woman, who

had been hungry, didn't get her dinner. He stood there, staring at Karen. "Uh," he tipped his hat with his free hand, "thank you, ma'am."

He turned, left the building and dropped the tacos in the nearest trash can. "Son of a bitch, Nick, you can't do anything right," he cursed himself out as he left the grounds.

CHAPTER THIRTY-EIGHT

The next morning the Chief arrived at the fairgrounds at nine in the morning. Just walking through the gate made him remember the blunder of last night. He took his hat off and rubbed his hand through his hair. There had been no reason to crack wise last night but there it was.

Now he was back to follow up on Analise. He was tempted to stop by the Exhibits building but he resisted the urge. No good would come of that. He hitched his equipment belt up and strode to the sandwich truck. Analise was sitting in the door of the truck, drinking a bottle of water. "Analise." He tipped his hat. The carnival music was already going. He wondered how the vendors and volunteers could take three days of that racket.

"Chief." She saluted him with the water. "What brings you out to the fair so early in the day?"

He waited until an elderly couple, the husband in a scooter, passed by. "I'm looking into Ina's murder. You're next on the list to be interviewed."

"I don't have a lot of time, Chief." She capped the bottle and stood on the top step of the fold down stairs leading into the truck. "I've got the noon food to prep."

"Just a few questions, Analise. When was the last time you saw Ina?" Nick pulled his notebook out of the front pocket of his uniform khaki shirt. He clicked the pen and looked at her expectantly.

She shrugged. "I don't know. Last winter, I guess. Arris and Ina were probably at a dance somewhere and I saw them. Who knows?" She turned and stepped up into the truck.

Nick followed her, mounting to the step she'd just left. He was just about inside the truck, and there was nowhere for Analise to go. He jotted a note. "Did you speak to Ina? Or Arris?"

"No." She began ripping a head of lettuce apart and putting the individual leaves into an rectangular aluminum container.

"Just no?"

"No, not really. I might have said hello to her in the ladies room. That's it. There was no reason to talk to Arris." She eyed Nick. "You do know Arris and I have been divorced for years, right? Why would I talk to either one of them?" She picked up a bulb of garlic and slammed it on the aluminum counter breaking the cloves apart. Analise picked up a knife.

"Do you know anyone that might have wanted to hurt Ina?"

Analise smashed a clove of garlic with the knife, startling Nick. He'd been writing and didn't see the loud bang coming.

"The woman was a bubble-head. You know, nothing but soap bubbles. There weren't enough

177

brains there to make her a threat to anyone."

"You think she threatened someone?"

The truck owner turned, knife still in hand, to face the Chief. She shook the knife at him. "Don't go puttin' words in my mouth, Nick White."

His face darkened. "Don't go wavin' a knife at me, Analise Van Horn."

She glanced at the knife in her hand and went pale. "Anyway," she went back to the garlic, "the woman was too stupid for words. I don't know what Arris saw in her."

"What about Arris?"

Analise sighed and rolled her eyes. "What about him?"

"Do you know anyone that would want to hurt Arris?"

"What a stupid question, Nick. Arris is just fine. Ina's the one who's dead."

"I know." He waited for the statement to sink in.

The chopping stopped halfway through the pile of garlic. "What do you mean?"

"I mean, would anyone want to hurt Arris?"

Nick saw her left eyebrow twitch. She began to chop the garlic with more energy than the tiny cloves warranted.

"Ridiculous. The man is infuriating. Way too in love with that miserable ranch. But why would anyone want to hurt him?"

Nick used the end of his pen to scratch his forehead. "That's what I'd like to know." He made a final note and clicked the pen closed. "Sorry to take up so much of your time, Analise. Have a good day today." He stepped down to the ground. "Oh, yeah." He turned back to look at the truck owner. "I had a report of you arguing with a couple of men, yesterday?"

He watched her throat work a swallow as her chopping stopped.

"So?" she glared at him, both hands on the stainless steel counter.

"Just wondered. Have to keep the peace, ya know. They causing you any trouble? You expect them back?"

Analise took a deep breath. "No, they're not causing me any trouble." She stood up. "I can take care of myself, Nick White."

"I'm sure you can, Analise." He tipped his hat and turned to leave. Before he'd gone ten feet, the door of the truck slammed shut.

He tucked the notebook into his shirt pocket. "Yep, Jean was right. There's something going on."

CHAPTER THIRTY-NINE

Jean walked around the livestock barns. Officer Tom trailed behind her. He had followed her home last night in his cruiser. She saw another officer, one she hadn't met, relieve him about seven pm. The new guy was still there in the morning but at 7am she'd seen Tom's cruiser pull up. She went to fix tea and breakfast, wondering if they should ride together. She'd decided against it by the time she finished dressing.

It was too much to just sit in the Exhibits building all day. She needed to get up and move around. She had her little Olympus camera with her. It was both waterproof and shockproof; she called it her hiking camera. It was several years old now, but she still loved the pictures it took and was used to the controls. Her son, Jim, often chided her about it.

"It's only got ten megapixels, Mom," he'd told her on a camping trip last year. "There are better cameras on the market now."

"Maybe so," she'd admitted. "But this one works

fine, it does everything I need it to do and I know the controls. I'll keep this one, thank you very much."

She snapped a picture of a young 4-H'er brushing her steer. The girl was being gentle and the animal stood still, eyes half closed as it chewed its cud. He obviously liked being groomed. Pictures like this would look great on the fair's website and social media page. She didn't worry about getting the parents' permission to use the photos. All 4-H members signed those waivers at the start of every year.

She walked around taking pictures of stall cleaning, goat watering and grooming, rabbits in their cages and chickens in all of their bizarre, feathered, top-knot finery. In the show ring, the FFA and 4-H kids were showing chickens. They were graded on how well they handled the birds and whether the chickens met the standards for their particular breed, among other things. Jean took some pictures of that show as well.

It was nearly ten o'clock when she wandered back to the Exhibits building. "Jean!" she was greeted as she walked in. Karen waved her over to where she was standing with her daughter and a young man. Jean tucked her camera away and went to join the group. "Glad you're back. You remember my daughter, Peggy?"

Jean shook hands. "I do. Nice to see you again, Peggy."

"And this is her friend, Tyler."

Jean studied his face. "Hello, Tyler. Nice to meet you."

"They're walking around the fair and stopped in to say hi, so I'm glad you got back in time."

"Enjoy the fair," Jean said.

"I'll see you tonight, Mom." Peggy gave her mom a kiss on the cheek.

"Have fun, you two." Karen waved to them as they wandered away.

"What's he do for a living?" Jean asked as they watched the pair look at the wood crafts halfway down the building.

"Odds and ends, handyman, nothing permanent." Karen sighed as she sat down and put her needlework in her lap. "Peg is studying to be a nurse. But now she's hooked up with Tyler I'm afraid he's going nowhere and will drag my daughter down with him."

"I've seen Tyler before." Jean drew the folding chair over to Karen and sat down. "He was arguing with Analise yesterday. I couldn't hear any of their conversation, though she was pointing at him and apparently reading him the riot act."

Karen stopped her needle in mid-air. She took a deep breath, eyes staring off to the end of the building. "He worked for her last winter. I don't know doing what, though. She doesn't run the truck in the winter but she does do catering." Karen looked at Jean. "Do you think he's involved in Ina's murder?"

"I don't know." Jean fussed with the scarf she had over her head. It was a patterned scarf she'd picked up during a cruise to the Caribbean. Brilliant red and yellow flowers on an orange background with green leaves made the scarf quite loud. Jean had never worn it after she'd bought it, it wasn't her style. It did complement the yellow sleeveless blouse she had on though, so she wore it today. I should go have the scarf vendor tie this for me, she thought as she tugged the nylon into place. "That's what I told the Chief last night right before he insulted me." Just thinking about his snarky comment made her angry.

"He stopped by last night, just after you left."

"That's too bad," Jean snapped.

Karen held up a hand. "I think he came by to apologize. He brought your tacos and my lemonade. A lemonade for you, too."

Jean crossed her arms over her chest. "I can't be bought with lemonade." She scowled. "I think Analise is in this up to her plucked eyebrows. I don't care what Mr. Snarky Police Chief has to say."

"I agree." Karen resumed her cross stitch work. "Too bad we can't ask her."

"Hmm," Jean agreed. "I've only talked to the woman a couple of times and both times she was less than friendly. Is she always like that?"

"Yep. I have no idea how Arris and Analise got together. Two totally different people. Following her around probably won't get us anywhere. She's here on the fairgrounds until closing. If she's like me, she just wants to go home, get a shower and drop into bed."

Jean sat forward, elbows on knees. "But she had that argument with Tyler yesterday. Maybe that's got her worried." Jean turned her head to look at her friend. "She may be goaded into doing something."

"Long shot, Jean. Tyler didn't seem uncomfortable when he and Peg came in to say hello. If he had a hand in the murder, I would think he'd act a little more antsy, especially here on the fairgrounds."

"True." Jean fussed with the scarf again. It was hot in the building and sweat was forming at her temples. She jumped up. "I'm going to go see if the scarf lady will re-tie this scarf for me."

Karen's eyes twinkled. "And then you're going to stand around where you can watch Analise, aren't you?"

"I am. Something is going on with that woman. I plan on figuring out what it is."

"Have fun. And stay out of trouble," Karen called after Jean.

Jean waved back. "Of course."

CHAPTER FORTY

Jean walked with Tom to the midway, telling him she was going to hang around there for awhile. He nodded and Jean smiled at his quiet sigh. At the scarf lady's stall she not only had the scarf she was wearing tied smartly, but she also bought a scarf in a beautiful jewel blue for Karen for a Christmas present. Afterward she took her bag and bought a lemonade from the stand next to Analise's sandwich truck. She chatted with the vendor for a bit, asking how this year's fair was working out for him. He was happy. The hot weather was driving lemonade sales up, and there seemed to be a lot of people on the midway. He thought it would be a good sales year for him.

She thanked him, then wandered to a picnic table where a nearby vendor had erected a canopy to provide shade. Jean sat at the far end of the table where she could see Analise's truck and stay in the shade, but not right out on the midway where she was easy to see.

Jean sipped her lemonade only occasionally. She

wanted to stay here and an empty cup would seem odd. Over the course of the rest of the morning, several people stopped and shared the table. An elderly couple sat down with iced tea to rest. A young family stopped by who needed a place to sit while Mom changed the baby's diaper and where the older child could enjoy her dish of ice cream. Jean was happy to hold the baby for the young woman as she dashed for more napkins and a bottle of water to wash the messy three-year-old's ice cream face and hands. It had been a very long time since Jim was a baby.

All the while, Jean watched the truck. The sandwich business was steady. Analise sold breakfast sandwiches until eleven, then she switched to a lunch menu. Jean saw her step out and change the signs on her truck. Peggy and Tyler walked by, not noticing Jean off to the side. Arm in arm, they passed the sandwich truck and Tyler never looked in that direction. Analise, who was in the service window watching the people walk by, saw him. The woman scowled but didn't say anything.

Well that was kind of a bust, Jean thought as Peggy and Tyler passed out of sight. If Tyler and Analise were in cahoots over Ina's murder, you'd think they'd be more nervous. She sucked up the last of the now watered-down lemonade. She pulled her phone out and dialed Arris.

"Hi, just calling to see how you're doing."

"I'm good. It's been kind of nice, having time to get some projects done around the ranch."

"I'll bet it is." She covered one ear with her hand to block out the carnival noise. "I wondered if you know what project Analise had Tyler Siddons doing last winter?"

There was a pause on the other end of the line. "I know she hired him for some catering work over the Christmas and New Year holidays. She does a lot of catering that time of year."

"How about in January or February?" Jean wasn't sure when Ina had died but it had to be about then.

"No, not that I know of. She likes to travel during those months. It's a slow period for her business."

Jean's hopes were dashed. "Thanks, Arris. I was just wondering. Karen just introduced me to the young man and I wondered how he and Analise were connected."

"He's a good enough boy, just no direction in his life. He's done some work for me now and then the last few years. Heavy stuff; some logging, replacing fence posts, that sort of thing. He likes to take a lot of breaks."

"I appreciate the information, Arris." She pondered his statement. "You think Tyler was upset with you at all?"

There was a long pause. "You're asking me if I was hard enough on him to set me up for a murder?"

"Yeah, I am. Were you hard on him?"

"Nah. Just told him the work wasn't going to do itself. I was working with him, Jean. Damn, if he was that mad, I think I'd have noticed. He's forty years younger than I am. I just nudged him along, is all."

She sighed. It seemed like a dead end. "I guess you're right. We all miss having you here."

"Once this clears up, I'll be back. It just seemed wrong to be under suspicion and running the fair."

"Understand, Arris. You made the right choice. Talk to you later, okay?"

"Sure, Jean. Don't forget to have fun."

She smiled. "Tyler do, Arris. Bye."

She clicked the off button on her phone. That didn't go the way she'd hoped. Jean got up and went to the lemonade guy to order two more drinks. Then she went to the sandwich truck window. "Hey, Analise. I'd like two sandwiches, please. A roast beef and a grilled chicken to go."

Analise glared but started working.

"How's business? Are you seeing enough traffic?"

Analise gave Jean a stare, then went back to making the order. "It's okay. Not great, but I'll do all right by the end of the fair."

"Glad to hear it."

Jean saw an eyebrow rise, but Analise kept working. Two teens stopped to read the menu sign. *There goes any chance of getting her to talk.* Analise wrapped the sandwiches and handed them down.

"Ten dollars."

Jean passed a ten dollar bill up. "Thanks, they look good. I saw you talking to Tyler Siddons the other day." She saw the woman freeze.

"And?"

"Oh, sorry. It looked like you two were arguing." *I won't tell her I was too far away to hear.* Jean could see her eyebrows draw together.

"He did some work for me over the holidays and claims I shorted him his pay."

"That's too bad." She gathered up the sandwiches. "Have a good day," Jean said brightly and walked away. She could hear the teens ask Analise for two subs.

That was a waste of time, Jean thought. *It was hard to tell if she's hiding something or just crabby all the time.* She went back to the Exhibits building and offered Karen her choice of the sandwiches and a lemonade. They'd have to think of something else to find out what Analise was doing.

CHAPTER FORTY-ONE

After they ate, Jean wandered around the Exhibits building. She could do some things but the wide array of crafts and skills made her feel both inadequate and envious. Jean stopped to admire one of the miniature gardens in the Floriculture department that sported a Best of Show ribbon. It was in a large shallow pottery bowl with three legs. In the bowl was a tiny fairy house made of twigs, a ceramic fairy standing outside of the door. A flat pebble had been placed at the door as a doorstep. Miniature daffodils stood like trees a quarter of the way around the bowl while moss had been used to line a winding stream that ran around the surface. A tiny wooden pole fence ran from the right side of the house across a third of the bowl, and grass was planted and trimmed to resemble a pasture. A porcelain cow stood in the middle of the field. Jean was enchanted and wondered where the creator found such a small recirculating pump for the stream. I could do something like this, she thought. Not with a pump though, just a cute little dish garden. She knew from chatter the last few days that the local nursery sold many pre-made items for miniature gardens and terrariums. *Maybe I'll try that, once things slow down a little.*

She found Chief White in the woodworking section, chatting with the volunteer on duty. The volunteer spotted a boy reaching out to pick up one of the displays. "Don't touch, please, young man," the elderly volunteer called out. The boy yanked his hand back and stared wide-eyed at the volunteer. "It's okay to look, son, we just don't want you to touch." He excused himself from Nick and walked over to the boy. "Would you like me to show you the piece?" The boy nodded and the man picked up the display and started to explain how it had been made.

Nick was watching the interaction and didn't see Jean. She thought about walking on by without speaking but the whole Analise thing was bugging her. "He's doing a good job," she said behind Nick.

He turned to see who was speaking. She was surprised to see a look of pleasure spread across his face. "Hi, Jean. What's that?"

Jean nodded toward the man and the boy. "That's part of what the volunteers are in here for, to encourage new crafters. The boy is interested, and the volunteer is feeding that interest."

"Oh, yeah, I see what you mean." He cleared his throat. "Uh, I wanted to say I'm sorry about yesterday. That comment didn't come out the way I meant it."

The reminder made her angry all over again. She reconsidered talking to him about Analise and Tyler. "It was snarky and mean-spirited, if that's what you mean." Jean saw him react as though he'd been slapped. "You aren't the only one in town with the ability to add one and one."

Nick hung his head and backed up a step.

"But, I'm willing to move past it if you are."

"I'd like that."

"Fine. I have another tidbit of information for you." She watched as his jaw worked under the skin. *He's going to blow this off, too. If it wasn't for Arris I'd walk off and leave this yokel to fail on his own.* She took a deep breath. "I called Arris. Seems Tyler Siddons has worked for Arris, on and off over the last few years. And Analise hired Tyler last winter for some work. I told you they'd argued in public. Anyway, I watched Analise this morning on the midway. She's hiding something. I don't know exactly when Ina was killed but they may have worked together at the time of Ina's disappearance." She jammed her hands into her shorts pockets and waited, watching his face.

"Well, uh, thanks for the information." He reset his hat and scuffed his boots on the cement floor. "I appreciate you bringing it to me."

"You don't think it's worth looking into, do you?" Jean was peeved and it came through in her voice.

Nick waited until a family of four passed them by. "I don't know, Jean. Tyler has been known to work for Analise from time to time, so I have no idea how significant it is that he worked for her last winter."

Jean could feel a trickle of sweat run down the middle of her back. She ground her teeth together. "Fine. I'll be on my way then." She stepped around him to go back to her usual spot.

"Jean, wait."

She turned around and stared him in the eyes.

"Uh, I do appreciate that you bring me these bits

of information. An investigator never knows where the key piece of info will come from."

"You're welcome," she said, though the words sounded as though they had been dipped in ice. She turned and left, annoyed that he'd blown her off again.

Two minutes later Jean slammed into the chair next to Karen. "He did it again."

"Who did what?" Karen put her cross-stitch down in her lap.

"Chief White. I just told him about Tyler and Analise and how she behaved all morning and he acted as though the info was useless." Jean yanked down on the front hem of her blouse to straighten it out.

Karen smoothed her piece of work. "It all may be nothing, you know that, Jean."

"Maybe," Jean snapped. "But he doesn't need to act as though I'm wasting his time."

A nod was the only response. Jean stewed for a minute. "I think, after we close up for the night, we follow Analise out of here and see where she goes. She was annoyed with me at lunch time. Maybe it's enough to goad her into making a mistake."

Karen's eyebrow arched. "Nine o'clock at night? Go snooping around behind Analise? Don't you think she'll go straight home?"

"Not if she has something to hide." Jean sat forward on her chair and faced her friend. "Look, if she really is involved in Ina's disappearance, she's going to want to cover up whatever loose ends are out there. I know I hit a nerve with her."

"Sure, why not. But how are we going to follow her when you have to lock up?" She nodded at

Officer Williams who was sitting in Jean's usual chair, chatting with a couple. "And what about him and the night shift? They're going to follow you around."

"Crap, I forgot about them." She stared at Tom. He was going to get off at seven tonight and meet his family at the gate for a Saturday night out at the fair. "Maybe I can slip the leash."

"How are you going to do that?"

"I'll go home, you follow Analise. I'll slip out, hop the backyard neighbor's little fence and go through their yard to the next block. I can call a cab and join you wherever you are." She grinned at the thought of outfoxing her babysitter.

"You look like a teenager about to sneak out of the house to meet her friends." Karen shook her head. "What if she goes way out of town?"

"Then we'll drop the whole thing. You can't go by yourself."

"Sounds shaky to me but yeah. Let's give it a try."

Jean hooted, drawing Tom's attention. She waved to him that everything was all right.

"You are incorrigible," Karen said with a laugh.

"It's been awhile since I've been naughty," Jean giggled back at her. "It feels kinda good."

CHAPTER FORTY-TWO

Nick stewed all the way back to his office. *Put your foot in it again, knothead. You could have been a little more enthusiastic about the news she gave you. You didn't know that Tyler had worked for Analise last winter. That's a good clue. You couldn't say so?* He smacked the steering wheel. *Now you've ticked her off again.* He pulled into the parking lot of the police station and slammed on the brakes as he pulled into his assigned slot. For good measure he slammed the SUV door and mashed the automatic door lock button hard enough to make his finger hurt.

Inside he nodded at the officer on duty behind the reception glass. Greta didn't work weekends so he had to unlock both the outer and inner doors to his office and, once inside, he tossed his hat on the hat rack and fell into his chair. Nick scrubbed his face with both hands. *What do I do next?* His brain whirled. *I've got bupkis as far as a real clue goes. Josh Marlow would be my guess as murderer. He's been on the wrong side of the law quite a few times, but only small-time stuff, nothing close to a murder charge. But he is a war vet and had the training. Maybe he snapped or something.*

He made a note to ask about the investigation into Marlow's fellow cowhands, then swore under his breath. It was the weekend, nothing was going to turn up until at least Monday. He tipped back in his chair, the soft leather creaking with his weight. His conversation with Analise this morning made him suspicious of her, too. But that didn't make any sense. Arris had gone out with plenty of women since the divorce. Analise had never kicked up too much fuss about any of them. Why would she kill Ina?

And what about Tyler Siddons? Nick didn't know of any trouble the young man had been in. He sat forward, turned on his computer and monitor and logged in. He pulled up the database and searched for Tyler Siddons. Nothing came up. There, he thought. No one goes from law abiding citizen to murderer without a very good reason. Still, there was the Analise and the Arris connections. Maybe he should call Tyler in for a chat.

He picked up the phone and dialed the officer on duty at the reception desk. "Get someone to call Tyler Siddons in for questioning concerning the Ina Grange investigation, would you?" The officer said he'd get right on it and Nick hung up the phone.

Nick spent a few minutes mulling over all of the different people involved in the investigation. He scratched at his chin. *I wonder if there's a connection between Analise and Josh Marlow? Or between Marlow and Siddons? Maybe all three are involved somehow?* He jotted some possible questions on a legal pad and resolved to stop by the fair and ask Analise a few more questions. He had a few for Marlow, too.

Nick picked up the phone again. "Get someone to call Josh Marlow in for questioning on the same case." He listened for a minute. "No, I don't want them to see each other. Make sure they come in separately." Nick hung up.

He tapped his fingers on the handset, then punched a speed-dial button.

"Paul?"

"Yeah, Nick."

"You have anything on the collection agencies?"

"Not yet. I've got calls in to four of them but it's the weekend. I probably won't hear back till Monday."

Nick ran his free hand through his hair. "Yeah. I was afraid of that. Same with Marlow's cowhand buddies, I suppose?"

"Yep. Sorry."

"That's okay. I'm just sittin' here trying to sort all of these clues out."

"Good luck with that. I finished talking to Ina's family. Ina's people knew about her gambling. They all said they tried to get her to go to Gambling Anonymous or to rehab but she refused to go. They were definitely suspicious of Arris. Called him a gigolo and were certain he was after her property. They admitted she was broke, so there's that."

"Thanks, Paul. Do you have that whole part of the investigation in a report yet?"

"Not yet. I'm in my garden, pulling weeds."

"Okay," Nick sighed. "I'm looking forward to some more tomatoes."

"I'll bring some in Monday. You should take the rest of the day off, Nick. Man, you work seven days a week."

"After this murder is solved, buddy."

#

Two hours later the light for the reception desk lit up as the phone rang. Chief White stopped reviewing reports and picked it up. "Yeah."

"Chief, we have Tyler Siddons in the interview room. Marlow isn't answering his cell but the ranch says he and the rest of the hands came into town mid-afternoon. I put a notice out to the patrols and I'll keep trying his number."

"Thanks. Appreciate that." Chief White hung up the phone. He reviewed the questions on his pad on his way to the interview room. Tyler Siddons was sitting at the middle of the small table facing the door when Nick opened it up. He pulled out one of the chairs on the door side of the table and sat down.

"Thanks for coming in, Tyler. I appreciate it."

Tyler glanced up at the cameras, one in each corner of the room facing him. "Sure, Chief. What's this all about?"

"You know about the Ina Grange murder?"

"Sure." Tyler shrugged. "News is all over town."

"We're trying to find out what happened and we're bringing a lot of people in, you know, to see if we can get it sorted out. Your name came up in a couple of interviews."

Tyler's blue eyes got big. "Me? How'd my name come up?"

"I was talking to Analise this morning. She said you worked for her last winter?"

The young man's face relaxed. "Yeah. Over the holidays I helped her with the catering, doing the scut

198

work, peeling, chopping, carrying trays and doing deliveries. I've done that the last couple of years."

Nick jotted a note and looked back up. "I heard you two got into an argument at the fairgrounds."

Tyler sat forward. "She stiffed me a week's pay. She had a big party to cater in February, a wedding, and she called me for help. I did my thing, she said she'd pay me when she got paid." He snorted. "She still hasn't settled up. That's what we were arguing about." He sat back in the chair. "Analise is always doing crap like that."

I told Jean that's probably what it was. He felt slightly vindicated as he took another note. "You know anything else about what Analise did all winter?"

"I know she took off after the wedding on a cruise. Probably with my money," Tyler added with a bit of venom.

"You don't know what she did between New Year's and the wedding?" Nick put on his friendliest face.

"Nah, I was cuttin' wood up on the rim all of January for Nate Brown. We musta cleared an acre a day. The guy's a slave driver."

Nick was disappointed. Tyler Siddons was turning into a dead end. "You know Josh Marlow?"

Tyler shook his head. "I've seen him at a few of the dances, but he's a lot older. I don't hang with his crowd."

Crap, Nick thought as he made one more note. *I was hoping there'd be a connection between those two.* He looked over his questions. This guy didn't seem to be a suspect. He stood up and held out his hand. "Thanks for coming by on a Saturday, Tyler. We're doing our best to clear up this thing. People get nervous about a murder in town."

Tyler stood up and shook his hand. "Glad to help, Chief."

Nick opened the door and stopped. "One more thing. Jean Hay's car was vandalized a couple of days ago. You know anything about that?

Tyler stopped short before bumping into Nick. Eyes wide, he shook his head. "No. I heard Karen Carver talk about it a day or so ago."

"Oh?" Nick closed the door. "What did Ms. Carver say?"

Tyler wiped his hand down the front of his shirt. "Just that it happened and Ms. Hays wasn't hurt."

"Anything else?" Nick deliberately stood close to Tyler, a trick he'd learned years ago.

"They wondered if Josh Marlow was involved."

"Really?" Nick nodded. "Go on."

Tyler backed up a step. "Ms. Carver said you got rid of stalking charges from him, that's all."

"I see. Did they speculate on anything else?"

The young man shuffled his feet. "Well, they wondered if Josh killed Ms. Grange."

"Uh huh. What do you think?"

Tyler swallowed. "Like I said, I don't hang with his crew."

"But?"

"Well, the guy is kind of crazy."

"Have you had a run-in with him before?"

"I saw him, one night in a bar. It was crowded and a guy bumped into him. Spilled his beer. Marlow had the man up against the bar and a knife at his throat before anyone knew what was goin' on. He's a scary dude."

"Hmm." Nick opened the door and walked Tyler

to the reception door. "We appreciate the help, Tyler." He showed the young man out and closed the door. "Any word on Marlow?" he asked the officer at the desk.

"Not yet, Chief. I'm still calling him every ten minutes. The phone isn't off, he just isn't answering."

"Keep on it."

"Yes, sir."

Nick went back to his office and re-read his notes for the whole case. Even with Tyler's information on Marlow's temper, he was getting nowhere, fast.

CHAPTER FORTY-THREE

Saturday afternoon went fast. A lot of people walked through the Exhibits building and conversations whirled around how to do this or that craft, how people could join various craft groups, and friends meeting friends in the aisles and having a chat. By eight that night, Jean was tired. She handed Karen a bottle of water; the building, despite the fans on high speed, was still stifling.

"Thanks." Karen uncapped the water and drank half of it in one long swig. "My throat was dry from all of the talking I've been doing all day."

Jean saluted her friend with her own bottle of water. I've decided to give John the keys to the building. He can lock up and we can leave on time and watch Analise."

"Good plan. I was wondering how we were going to get out in time to catch her. We may have to stay in the parking lot awhile though. If she has customers, I don't think she's going to cut them off."

"Oh, I hadn't thought of that. You're right." Jean

sank down on the second chair in Homemaking Arts. "I've been thinking about Analise, Tyler, Arris and Ina all day. Everyone is connected. Josh Marlow, too, at least through Ina."

"It's a small town, Jean. If you grew up here you know all of the old families."

"I wonder if Josh knows Analise?"

"He does. Josh and Analise were an item a couple of years ago. All the tongues were wagging over how she was dating a younger man. By the time Josh and Ina were an item, the novelty had worn off."

Jean stared at her friend, mouth hanging open. "You never told me that."

Karen stopped the bottle of water halfway to her mouth. "I didn't? Sorry. It's hard to remember you're new here and not up on all of the past gossip."

"That may make a difference." Jean slumped back in her seat. "We were going at Josh all wrong, asking him about Ina. Maybe we should have been asking about Analise?"

"Could be. If you pressed her hard enough, do you think she'd meet with Josh?"

Jean stuck a finger up under the scarf and gently scratched her head wound. "We can hope so."

CHAPTER FORTY-FOUR

Nick was just finishing up his reports when the desk officer came in. "The lab sent this to our printer, Chief." He passed his boss a handful of papers.

"Thanks." Nick turned his desk light back on and sat down as the officer left.

He read through the report fast, then went back to the first page and read it all again, taking in all of the information. When he finished, he flopped back in his desk chair. Marlow's fingerprints were on Jean's car from the slashed tires case. *And we haven't found the guy all day.* He rubbed his eyes. Too damn much paperwork, he mused. So, if Marlow slashed her tires, was he also the one who attacked her in the fair parking lot?

He shook his head. There was no connection between the two crimes but who else would be angry enough at the woman to do those things? Where is this guy? He picked up the phone and called the desk.

"I want Josh Marlow found for questioning on the slashed tires case. We're no longer just bringing him in for friendly questioning. I want him in here as soon as he's found." Nick listened to the officer's confirmation and hung up. He drummed his fingers on top of the fingerprint report. Marlow was looking more and more like a suspect but something wasn't right. He wished he could put a finger on what was bothering him about the case.

CHAPTER FORTY-FIVE

The two women left the Exhibits building at 8:55 pm. "Here's what we'll do. I'll drive home," Jean told Karen in a whisper as they walked to the parking lot. Jean's night escort was twenty feet behind her. "You'll watch Analise. Call me on my cell as soon as you see her leave and stay on with me until you get to where she's going." They arrived at their cars. "I'll sneak out and get to you as soon as you've stopped."

Karen nodded. "Okay." She looked past Jean as she gave her a hug. "The officer is getting into his car. I'll keep you posted."

The women split up and Jean drove home. She fumbled in the rental car for the light switch. "I'll be glad when I get my own car back," she grumbled when she finally found the switch. *I hope it doesn't rain before then, I'll never be able to find the wipers.* The drive home was uneventful. She pulled into the carport and saw the officer park on the other side of the street and turn off his lights. Jean hadn't said more than hello to the young man since her police escort had been put on her. She imagined it must be boring as hell to sit there all night in the dark without even a book to read.

In the house she turned on the living room light and the bedroom light. Karen called. "Analise has come out of the fair and got in her car. I'm following her right now."

"Thanks, Karen. Any idea where she's headed?"

"Not yet, but I don't know where she lives so we could be wrong and the woman is just going home."

Jean set the cell phone on the bathroom sink counter and splashed her face. It felt good to get the heat, sweat and dust of the day off of her skin. She picked up the phone. "Can I grab something from the fridge for a snack for you?"

"A cold cola would be good, if you have any."

"I think I have some from the night I had you and the girls over for dinner. I'll look."

Jean went downstairs and turned on the kitchen light. Way in the back, on the bottom shelf, she found a six-ounce can of cola. "Hey, I found you one," she said into the cell phone.

"Good. A little shot of caffeine will help me stay awake. Nothing to report yet except we're headed into the southwest corner of town. It's all residential over here. I think she's headed home."

"She may be meeting someone at her house." Jean turned off the light in the kitchen and in the living room. Once in the bedroom she put the can of soda in her purse, then changed her mind. She walked over to her closet and began to rummage around on the shelf over the clothes pole. Ha, she cheered to herself. Gotcha. Jean pulled a small daypack down and took it to the dresser. She pulled wallet, the soda, a tiny flashlight and a pocket knife from her purse and put them in the daypack. *Much better, now I'll have my hands free.* She put the pack on her back and turned off the bedroom light. It took a couple of minutes for her eyes to adjust to the dark.

She didn't want to use the flashlight, that would look suspicious to the cop stationed outside. In the living room she opened the sliding patio door and stepped out into the night. After she pulled it closed she realized there was no way to lock the door. She agonized for a moment, then shrugged. There was a cop watching her house. The house would probably be safe enough unlocked. At the back of her property she climbed over the rail fence that divided her neighbor's yard from hers. Moving along the right edge of the property, she made her way to the street on the next block.

Her heart beat fast and she was breathing hard as she walked along the sidewalk to the corner, then away from her house. The night was beautiful. The sky was awash with stars and Jean could pick out the major constellations. It was about eighty degrees so she didn't have on a sweater or jacket. Sneaking out of the house was quite exciting.

Karen spoke. "We must be at her house. She pulled into the garage and shut the door."

"I'm out of my house. Where are you?"

Karen gave her the address. "Be careful. Get out on the corner of Chestnut and Pine. Walk up. I'll be parked on the right side of Pine before you get to her house."

"Gotcha. I'll call a cab and be there as quick as I can."

She called the only taxi company in town and

waited. Ten minutes later a cab pulled up to the street. Jean got in the back and gave him the address. He pulled out. "Nice night," he said in a conversational tone.

Jean nodded. She didn't expect the guy would chat, but why wouldn't he, trapped in the car for hours on end? "Yeah, nice night, especially after the heat of the day."

He looked at her in the rearview mirror. "You're not dressed for a party."

Her heart thumped. "No. My car's in the shop and a friend is sick."

"Oh, I'm sorry to hear that."

"Yeah. Nothing bad but she needs a hand."

"Nice of you."

Jean felt sick about the lie. "Just trying to help."

The taxi let her out on the corner and she gave him a five as a tip to soothe her conscience about the lie. She waited until he drove off to walk up Pine Street. Karen was in her car, a short distance away, the driver and passenger windows open to the soft night air. Jean knocked on the car door.

Karen jumped. "Oh my God, you scared me."

"Sorry." Jean got in the car and pulled the door closed until she heard the latch click. "What have you seen so far?"

"The lights were on when she got here." Karen looked from the house to Jean in the dim light of the street light on the corner behind them. Analise lived about the middle of the block. Another street light was two corners away in front of them.

Jean mulled that over for a second. "You think someone was already in the house?"

"I do. I have no idea who it might be. There's no

rumor around town that Analise is seeing anyone."

Jean looked at the house. It was a modern ranch-style home. A gabled roof covered the front entryway. The pillars and the front of the house were covered in a rough stone facing of local rock. Like the majority of houses in Greyson, the yard was covered in one-inch sized pieces of local granite; a big Manzanita tree was the centerpiece of the small front yard. A six-foot-high wooden privacy fence ran from the front left corner of her house to the neighbor's fence. Another one ran from the right front corner to her other neighbor's fence. Light showed dimly in the living room picture window.

"Do you think she has the blinds drawn or is she at the back of the house?"

"Back of the house, the kitchen, most likely."

"I wish I could see what's going on. There's no shouting that I can hear."

"I know."

Jean pulled the can of soda out of her daypack and handed it to Karen. "Oh, here's your drink."

The can snapped and fizzed when Karen pulled the tab. Jean could smell the beverage and Karen drank. "Oh, that hits the spot."

"Glad I could make your night." Jean studied the fence. "There's a gate on the left."

Karen turned to look at her. "You want to sneak into the backyard?"

"We're here to see what she's doing, right?" Jean wagged her eyebrows. "Well, let's do it."

It took a minute for Karen to agree. "This is going to end badly, I can just feel it."

"Nonsense. We'll be quiet as little church mice on Sunday. I just want to hear what's going on in there and maybe find out who else is in there."

"Fine." Karen drew in a deep breath. "Let's do this and go home."

Jean opened her door and slipped out onto the sidewalk, cursing the dome light for coming on. Karen slipped out too and both women closed their doors as quietly as they could. "Come on," Jean whispered as she came around the car.

The women hurried across the road and onto Analise's yard. The rock crunched under their feet. It sounded very loud to Jean. Her head swiveled in every direction to spot trouble. They made it to the gate and paused to still their racing hearts. "We're going to get caught," Karen whispered.

Jean examined the gate. "No we're not. There's no latch on the outside."

Karen rose up on tiptoe and reached over the top. They heard a metallic click. "It's on the inside. My gate works like this, too." The gate swung out toward them. Jean went in with Karen following. "I'll just pull it almost closed. We can get out in a hurry if we have to."

Rock covered the yard at the end of the house and Jean silently groaned. They'd be crunching every step of the way. She could see a bit of light at the back of the house. There were no windows at the end except a bathroom window fifteen feet up the wall. That was a relief. She waved to Karen and they crept toward the back yard. Jean peeked around the corner. Light was streaming out of a kitchen window onto a stone-paved patio. She eased around the corner.

It seemed that Analise used the square-foot gardening method. The backyard was a maze of garden beds. Tomatoes overran one four-foot square.

Squash vines spread out from another. Rose bushes lined the fence at the back of the yard. Everything was trim and tidy. She moved under the kitchen window, the light streaming out a foot over her head. Karen moved behind her.

"I can hear voices," Karen breathed.

Past the kitchen window the patio extended out into the yard; light came from there, too, illuminating redwood patio furniture. Jean inched to the corner and looked around. The patio blinds were open. Analise was inside the breakfast area sitting at the table with Josh Marlow. Jean ducked back. "It's Analise and Josh at the table."

In the dim light Jean could see Karen shake her head. "This is a bad idea."

"The door is open, just the screen door is closed. We can hear them." Jean was excited. Despite her racing heart and sweaty palms, she was having fun. She eased closer to the corner, Karen right behind. The two women, Jean low and Karen high, inched their heads around the corner so they could see and hear.

Analise had a glass of iced tea in front of her on the table. Josh had a bottle of beer. "So that's all you've done all day? Watch TV and drink beer? What about Miss Nosypants, Jean Hays?"

"Don't know," he snarled. "The cops have been calling my phone all day. I stayed here, out of sight. If you want something done about her, do your own dirty work." He raised the bottle and drained it, then scraped the chair across the sand-colored tiles and went to the kitchen.

Jean and Karen could hear the fridge open and a bottle top get twisted off and tossed onto a counter.

He sauntered back to the table and sat down, sprawled in the wooden chair as though he owned it. "What did you do all day? You're at the fair where she is."

"I worked. Something I recommend for you. You're never going to amount to anything."

Josh slammed the bottle on the table. "Watch your mouth!" He pointed at her nearly all the way across the table.

She laughed. "Don't threaten me, bucko." Analise took a sip of iced tea. "What do the cops want?"

"I don't know, now do I, since I didn't pick up." He sat back and took another pull on the beer. "But I bet it's about Ina. White came out to see me once already. I'll just bet he has more questions."

Analise sighed. "This is not working out."

"No kidding."

That's when Karen sneezed. Jean saw both heads swivel toward the door before she yanked her head back around the corner and ran as quietly as she could after Karen, who was already around the end of the house and running to the gate. Jean could hear the sliding screen door open and Josh come out onto the patio. She rounded the corner to the end of the house just before the patio light came on.

Karen was already through the gate and halfway across the front yard when Jean cleared the gate and shut it as softly as she could. Karen was starting the car when Jean reached the street. Jean opened the car door, jumped in and whispered, "Go!" She shut the door as Karen hit the gas. Jean turned to look behind them as the seatbelt bell dinged insistently. "Make the first turn, Karen, I don't care where it goes."

She rolled a little as Karen made a left. Jean could

see Josh out on the street staring at the car. Jean turned to face the front and put on her seatbelt so the damn bell would stop pinging. "Josh came out to the street but I don't think he could see anything but taillights. Hoo, that was close."

"Sorry about the sneeze. Something in that garden set my allergies off." Karen had a death grip on the steering wheel as she looked straight ahead, shoulders hunched forward.

"It's okay." Jean settled into the car seat. "I just wish we'd heard something important."

Karen took a deep breath and tried to relax her shoulders. "We heard that they're working together."

"True." Jean nodded. "There is that." She gave what she'd heard some thought. "Also, the police are trying to find him. That's an interesting fact as well."

Karen eased her grip on the steering wheel. "I think I've reached my limit for tonight's adventure. Ready to go home?"

"Yeah." Jean was thinking about Josh and Analise and what they could be up to. "Drop me a block away. I have to sneak back into the house."

The two women were silent the rest of the ride to Jean's house.

CHAPTER FORTY-SIX

The next day Jean was in the large livestock barn taking pictures of cattle when she ran into Arris. "Hello!" She beamed as she gave him a hug. "I'm so glad to see you."

"Nice to see you, too. How's the fair going?" He leaned against the gate of a cattle pen and put his boot up on the lower rail.

"I'm good. It's good. There seems to some sort of major problem every day but so far, it's nothing I can't handle. How are you?" The two pressed in against the gate as a 4-H girl dressed in her show uniform—a white shirt with green ribbon tie—walked a Black Angus cow down the aisle.

"I'm fine. My grandniece is showing today. I came down to cheer her on."

Jean nodded at the steer in the pen, lying down and half asleep. "This hers?"

He nodded. "She's worked so hard on her handling skills. I think she'll get a Grand Champion ribbon and a belt buckle this year."

"I wish her luck."

She fidgeted, a little uncomfortable about the question she wanted to ask, but since he was right here, she went ahead. "May ask about your break-up with Analise?"

A look of resignation crossed his face. His eyes focused on the other side of the barn where two young men in FFA jackets were cleaning out a pig stall. "Sure, why not?"

"I'm sorry, Arris. I'm just trying to make sense of this."

"That's all right. I'm not sure what you want to know. We've been divorced for years. No kids."

"Forgive me for prying, but who's your beneficiary?" She grew hot with embarrassment. "You know, in case of..." she struggled to find a polite way of putting it, "...an accident."

He nodded. "Analise. I keep meaning to change my will and give the ranch to my nieces and nephews." A sigh escaped. "But that's not something a mortal man wants to think about so I keep putting it off."

"I apologize for bringing up something so personal. I keep going over everything in my mind and nothing makes much sense. I wondered if there was a money angle."

"Ina had some money. Less than most people think because of the gambling."

He took his foot off of the bar and shifted his weight, putting the other boot up. He sighed. "Anyway, I have the ranch, and a pension from the power company. I received an inheritance a few years back. I'm comfortable but not a millionaire. Wouldn't be anyone interested in what I have."

Jean itched under her scarf, a sky blue cotton one today, the last day of the Fair. The gash on her head itched all of the time. She supposed that meant it was healing well but it was maddening. It occurred to her that she didn't suspect him of the murder. "I wish I could think of something, Arris. It's been a distracting week."

He wiped his forehead with his arm and reset his hat. "That it has." He looked at her scarf. "I was sorry to hear about the attack on you. How are you doing?"

"I'm fine. It itches though."

He laughed. "I had a steer gore me in the head back in my younger days, big gash right across my skull. Bled like nobody's business."

A grin spread across her face. "I'm in good company then." She gave him another hug. "I've got to get back to the Exhibits building. You take care of yourself."

He tipped his hat to her. "I'll do that."

#

Jean left the livestock barn and decided to walk around the fair through the midway to the Exhibits building. She bought a cup of iced tea from a vendor and sat down at the same picnic table she'd sat at the day before. Analise was doing a moderate business selling breakfast sandwiches as Jean sipped her tea. She pulled out her phone and dialed the Police Station.

"I'd like to speak with Chief White, please. Jean Hays."

"Ms. Hays, the Chief isn't in the office right now. May I take a message?"

"Yes. Ask him to call me when he gets a chance, would you?"

"Yes, ma'am. I'll give him the message."

She clicked off and sighed. She wished she had asked Arris about any near misses or accidents that happened to him recently. Then she wondered: would Analise kill for Arris's assets? She didn't know how big the ranch was but an acre of land in this area was going for five to twenty-five grand an acre depending on its location and ease of building. A nice ranch halfway up the rim might make a good development for vacation homes or something and be worth top dollar. She'd never been to his ranch but it seemed a shame that good farmland be built over for homes only used a few weeks a year.

Did Analise, crabby as she was, seem capable of killing someone? The bit of conversation Jean had heard between Analise and Josh the night before was inconclusive. They had something going on and they thought she knew something about it. Jean wished she *did* know what they were doing. Had Analise been talking to Josh when she'd said, "Take care of it," on the phone two days ago? It would make Jean feel a lot safer if she could predict what was coming next.

Jean rattled the ice around in the drink. It had been foolish to go to Analise's house last night. If they'd been caught and Josh and Analise were killers, well... She shuddered. She'd put Karen in a hell of a spot and only luck got them out. But, if Analise *was* after her ex's money, why didn't she kill *him*? Why Ina? Jean drank more of the tea as she watched Analise take orders and prep for lunch, just an hour away. She wondered what the laws in Arizona were for inheriting from someone convicted of murder. Her phone ringing made her jump. "Hello?"

"Jean, it's Nick White returning your call."

"Hi, Nick. Yes. I have a tiny bit of information to share."

"Go ahead."

She detected a bit of reluctance but she decided to ignore it. "I was talking to Arris this morning. His niece is showing her steer today."

"Yep."

"Well, he mentioned that Analise is still his beneficiary."

There was a pause on the other end. "For his estate?"

"That's what he said." She had to put a hand over her open ear to cut the music from the carnival so she could hear Nick.

"Interesting. Anything else?"

Now she felt as though she was on rocky ground. "I heard Analise and Josh Marlow talking last night."

He came back immediately. "Where'd you see Marlow?"

"Uh," she hesitated. Nick was going to be upset. "Uh, at Analise's house."

"You were at Analise's? Alone?"

"Oh, no. Karen was with me."

"Why'd Analise invite you to her house?"

Here it comes. Jean braced herself. "Well, she didn't exactly invite us."

"What do you mean, exactly?" He had the same tone of voice he'd used the day he called her to tell her about Marlow's stalking complaint.

"We... snuck into her backyard and overheard a conversation," she blurted out fast to get it over with.

"What?" Nick yelled into the phone.

Jean jerked it away from her ear. "We followed her home. Noticed the lights were already on when she got there. So we went to the backyard to see who she was meeting with."

"Are you crazy? Didn't I specifically tell you to leave the investigating to the police?"

She squinted her eyes shut, regretting the stupid move. "I know. We were almost caught when Karen sneezed."

"Oh for…" There was a long pause. Jean could hear him take a deep breath.

His voice was almost calm when he asked, "And what did you hear?"

"Two things." She was glad she didn't have him in person in front of her. "We heard Analise ask about Miss Nosypants. Meaning me. Josh said he stayed at her house all day."

"The second thing?" Nick's tone of voice brooked no nonsense.

Jean felt as though she were standing in front of her commanding officer or First Sergeant for a bad project. "Well, he said the cops had been calling his phone all day. That's why he didn't do anything about me."

The pause on the phone went on for so long Jean thought the connection had been lost. "I'm looking for Josh Marlow now," Nick finally said. "Don't do anything stupid today." He clicked off.

After a flash of annoyance about being told not to do anything stupid, a wave of both relief, then embarrassment washed over her. *He's right, we could have messed up his investigation.* She got up from the picnic bench and got two lemonades, one for herself and one as an apology to Karen. She started to walk by Analise's truck then thought better of it. No sense teasing the dog, she thought. She walked the long way around the fairgrounds, Officer Williams trailing behind her.

CHAPTER FORTY-SEVEN

It was mid-afternoon and the day was not only hot but sticky, too, as moisture built up in the atmosphere. "We may get a monsoon storm before sundown," Karen said. The two women were at the east end of the building, just outside the door, looking at the black thunderclouds building up in the sky over the Mogollon Rim to the north. "I hate it when it gets this humid."

"Better than the east coast. I've seen days back there the humidity was over ninety percent."

"That's why I live in Arizona," Karen quipped. "Over fifty is too much."

They went back into the building. Everyone was moving in slow motion. Men and women were using their fair maps to fan themselves. Children's hair was plastered to their heads with sweat. "This has been fun," Jean said as they walked back to the center of the building, "but I'll be glad when it's over. It's exhausting."

"True, but in a month we'll be starting to talk

about next year's fair."

They sat down in Karen's area and they each picked up a fair book and began to fan themselves. Jean's phone rang. "Yes?"

"There's a fight at the beer tent."

Jean gasped. "Did you call 911?"

"Yeah. I just hung up."

"Okay. I'll be right over." She clicked off and leapt out of her chair. "Tom," she called over to her police escort. He was pulling a bottle of water out of the cooler. "There's a fight at the beer tent."

She took off out of the center door with him beside her. They raced around the arena where the horse dressage competition was going on and to the west end of the midway where the beer tent was located. "911 has been called, a car is on its way," she told him as they ran. As they approached, they could see parents hustling kids away from the action. A large crowd circled whatever was going on in the area outside the beer tent entrance.

Tom pulled his badge from his belt and began to yell. "Police! Step back, clear the way." He pushed through the crowd, Jean on his heels.

Once in the middle they could see two men fighting. Jean wiped the sweat that ran down the side of her face. Both men were dressed in western shirts, one dark green, one medium blue, and both in blue jeans with cowboy boots. Their hats lay in the dirt, one on each side of the circle the crowd formed around the fighters.

The men were covered in dirt, blood streaming from a split lip on Blue Shirt and a cut over the eye on Green Shirt. Jean saw Tom head straight into the fight.

"Break it up!" he yelled. "Police, break it up, you two!" He stepped in to push them apart just as Blue Shirt took a swing at Green Shirt. It caught Tom on his jaw, spinning him around and sending him to one knee.

Jean found herself charging into the middle of the circle. She screamed, "As you were!" and ran to Tom's side. Tom was struggling to his feet. The two fighters paused to stare at her. After checking on the police officer she rounded on the two young men. "You should be ashamed of yourselves!" She shook her finger at them. "This is Sunday! This is a family event! Shame on you!"

The crowd began to laugh. The men wiped the blood from their faces as they looked around the circle of people.

"You're scaring the kids. Is this how you'd want your mother or grandmother to see you?"

They two fighters had the grace to look sheepish.

"Well?"

"No ma'am," Blue Shirt mumbled.

"No ma'am." Green Shirt shook his head.

Jean could hear sirens coming their way. Tom began to break up the crowd. The two men picked up their hats. "Don't go anywhere," she told them. "Walk right on over there." She pointed to the front of the beer tent. "Stand in the shade and wait. Officer Williams is going to ask you a few questions." The two young men walked over to the tent, heads hung and slapping the dirt off of their jeans with their hats.

"Are you all right, Tom?" Jean checked his face. "Ouch. That is going to leave a bruise."

"I'll be fine, Jean. Let me go take care of these yahoos."

She nodded. "Go ahead. I'll stay right here. In the shade, though."

He grinned and walked over to the cowboys.

A patrol car pulled up to the fence and Jean went over and unlocked the gate there. She stood near it but left it open so the police could get in and out. A few minutes later, an SUV pulled up. She watched Chief White get out. He stopped at the gate. "Everything under control?"

"Yep. Tom has them over there." She pointed at the three officers standing in front of the two fighters. "He got clocked on the chin. You may want to make him get it looked at."

"Will do."

He walked over to the officers. Jean stayed in the shade as much as she could. More and more clouds filled the sky. The pre-storm breeze was a welcome relief. Fifteen minutes later Nick came back to the gate. He gave her a stern look. "Officer Williams said you stopped the fight."

She shook her head. "No. He did. They stopped fighting when they realized they'd hit a cop."

"That's not the story I got from him or the cowboys." He continued to eye her.

He's going to think I'm a nut. Always barging into things I shouldn't be. She shrugged. "I gave them a scolding, that's all." She folded her arms over her chest. "Just reminded them of their behavior."

He cocked an eyebrow at her. "If that's how you want to see it." He went back through the gate. Halfway to his car, he stopped and turned back to her. "We have a suspect on your car tire slashing."

Jean turned around to look. "You do?"

"Yep. We haven't made an arrest yet though. I'll

keep you posted."

"Thank you. I appreciate it."

He tipped his hat and got into the car. She watched him drive off and grinned to herself. *This is great news. I can get my car back.*

CHAPTER FORTY-EIGHT

When she got back to the Exhibits building, Jean told Karen the latest from Chief White.

"Oh!" Karen gave her a hug. "That is great news. What happened at the beer tent?" Karen looked around. "And where is he?"

"Two cowboys were in a fight in front of the beer tent. It looked like half the people here were standing in a circle cheering them on."

"There's at least one fight there every year, usually on Saturday night, though, not Sunday afternoon." Karen sat down next to her and drank some water.

"Maybe because it's so hot. Everyone's a little cranky when it gets like this."

"Could be." Karen began fanning herself with her copy of the fair book.

"I'm going to go splash my face," Jean said as she got up. "I'll be right back."

After she went to the ladies' room she went outside the east-end door to look at the weather. The sky was black and she could hear thunder. Lightning was flashing to the north. John Gonzales stepped up beside her. "Looks like it's going to really monsoon. This time of day we usually have a lot of people in here. They come to see the fair and hang around to pick up their exhibits, but today the building is just about empty."

"The wind is really picking up. What should we do? Anything we should prepare?"

"Let's turn off the fans and close the louvers. That'll be a good start. We won't have to worry about the rain pounding in from there while we close the doors."

"Good plan, John. Can you get the fan on this end? I'll go take care of the other end."

"Sure, Jean."

She hurried to the other end of the building to turn off the fan and found the control to close the big metal louvers on the outside. She found the nearest Superintendent and warned him about the weather. Even with the fans off, lightweight displays were already starting to blow around in the breeze blowing through the building.

Jean had seen her first monsoon in July. She was used to rain, having grown up and lived on the East Coast. It could pour over there, it could rain for days, but a monsoon was different. In this area rain generally came from the north and east or north and west. Starting in July, the weather tended to come up from the Gulf of Mexico. And when it hit, the thunder rattled the windowpanes and water came out of the sky as if from a fire hose. Streets flooded; normally dry water channels throughout the town became raging rivers. All traffic stopped until the rain cleared. Half an hour after that the roads cleared of water and life could go on.

She went to Karen. "A monsoon is blowing in. I'm going to half close this side door. Hopefully I can keep most of the water out." Jean walked over and pulled the door half closed. People were leaving the building and no one was coming in. She stood and looked at the sky, enjoying how much it had cooled down.

Jean turned and went into the building, ready to sit down with Karen and enjoy the quiet and the cool air.

"You bitch!" Jean heard from behind her. She started to turn when a hand grabbed the back of her blouse and whipped her around. Jean found herself face to face with a furious Analise, a knife inches from her face. She could feel the adrenaline flood through her system.

The woman grabbed the front of Jean's blouse and pulled her in close. "This is your fault. Sticking your nose in where it doesn't belong." Analise waved the knife at her.

Jean's mouth went dry. As if from a distance, she could hear Karen cry out.

"Analise." Jean was surprised her voice worked. "Let's calm down. What's going on?"

"You... you bitch." Analise's blue eyes were wide and wild. A sheen of sweat covered her face. "You just couldn't leave things alone. You must be sleeping with him, otherwise why would you get involved?"

Jean blinked. "Wait, Analise. What are you talking about?"

The knife tip touched Jean's throat. "Don't play coy with me." Spittle gathered at the corners of Analise's lips. "You and Arris are trying to cheat me."

Jean's head was buzzing. She couldn't take her eyes

off of the foam in the corner of the other woman's mouth. "I didn't…"

"Yes, you did! Don't try and deny it. You're after the money. Admit it!" Analise pressed the knife against Jean's throat.

"Drop the knife, Analise!"

Jean tore her eyes away from Analise's face, just inches from her own. Ten feet away, Nick White was standing just inside the building door, gun pointed at Analise's back. Jean could feel her legs start to tremble. *Do not faint, Jean. Do not faint.*

"You heard me, Analise. Drop the knife. Let Ms. Hays go."

Jean saw him take a step forward just as Analise let go of Jean's shirt and slid her thin, ropey arm around Jean's neck. The woman moved in behind her somehow managing to keep the knife pressed against her throat.

"The money is mine, Chief. I put up with that man for years. Stupid ranch, he just wouldn't let it go!"

"Turn her loose, Analise. We can talk about it." Nick took another step forward.

Jean could see officers, including her former shadow, Tom Williams, approaching from both ends of the building. Her brain started to work. Analise was actually smaller than Jean, older and thinner. *What if I just drop and roll, or twist and roll? I might not get cut with the knife too much.* She swallowed, and another flood of adrenaline rushed through her.

"Don't be stupid, Nick. That's not like you at all." Analise's voice was right in Jean's ear.

Nick stood up, holstered his weapon and held his hands out to his sides. "Look, Analise. We'll just talk. Tell me the plan. Did you kill Ina?"

Analise's arm pressed tighter into Jean's throat. It was getting harder to breathe. *If I don't do something soon I'm going to pass out from lack of oxygen.* Jean glanced at the officers approaching from both directions. To her right, Jean could see Karen herding fair-goers toward the end door.

"No, I didn't. I hired Josh and Martin to do it. I should have done it myself."

"What was the plan, Analise?" Nick took another step forward.

Jean wondered how he was keeping his face so friendly.

"Arris would get blamed and go to prison. The property would come to me. I'd sell it and get the hell out of this backwater dump. I could be on TV, on the Cooking Network or something. Have a big, famous restaurant. But no. The man wouldn't sell."

"That's a shame, Analise. You do make a mean sandwich." Nick took another step forward.

Jean was getting dizzy from the pressure on her neck. She had to do something soon.

"I do. Don't I?"

The pressure on Jean's neck eased just a little, and that was the moment she decided to go for it. She grabbed Analise's arm and moved it just enough to twist to her left, away from the knife. Analise tried to regain her grip but slipped, dragging her fingernails across Jean's neck as she twisted away and dropped to the floor in a roll.

Jean could feel Nick rush up behind her. As she rolled to a stop, she saw Nick grab Analise's knife hand and twist it behind her. The knife dropped with a clang on the cement floor. Two officers rushed to Nick to take Analise while Officer Tom Williams helped Jean to her feet.

"Are you okay?" He winced when he looked at her neck.

"Um. Yeah. I think so."

He walked her to her chair by the door. "Let me get a medic in here. You're scratched up pretty bad."

Jean's head was buzzing. She touched her neck and stared at the blood on her fingers. Karen rushed up.

"Oh my God, Jean! Are you all right?" Her face was white and full of worry.

Jean felt as though everything was distant. "Yeah, sure."

An EMT arrived. "Hey, Ms. Hays. Remember me? I took care of you a few days ago."

Jean blinked. "Yeah. You bandaged my thumb."

"That's me." He pulled a flashlight from his breast pocket and flashed it in her eyes. "Did you hit your head, Ms. Hays?"

"No." She shook her head. "My neck is scratched, that's all."

He put the light back in his pocket. "Nasty things, fingernail scratches. Let's take a look."

Jean watched as two officers took Analise out of the side door. The woman glared at her but with an officer on each arm, there wasn't much else she could do. Jean could feel herself start to shake. "I think the adrenaline is making me sick."

"I imagine so, Ms. Hays." He pulled antiseptic and bandages and gauze from his kit and began working on her neck.

"Hold up, Mike."

Nick came up with an officer with a camera. "Let us get a couple of pictures of the scratches before you fix them."

Mike nodded. The officer stepped in, took a couple of pictures and hurried off. The EMT went back to work.

"How you doing, Jean?" She watched him trade glances with Karen.

"A little shaky, but I'm fine."

He nodded. "Good move, dropping and rolling like that. It let us get to her without hurting you. Too much," he added belatedly, after a glance at the EMT working on her neck.

"Glad I could help."

Karen rested her hand on Jean's shoulder, patting it with her fingers. Nick looked at her. "Can you get her home?"

"Sure. Not a problem."

"Good work, Jean." He nodded and went out the door. The rest of the officers were in the process of taking pictures of the scene and generally milling around.

"Looks like there's going to be a delay in exhibit pick-up." Jean nodded at the confusion in the middle of the building.

"Yeah, but people will get a big, juicy tidbit of gossip to share." Karen chuckled. "Don't you worry about it."

CHAPTER FIFTY

The next day, Jean met Karen at the Exhibits building. The doors were open, everything gone but the permanent stands. Jean pulled the plastic bins with left over ribbons out from under the display stand where she had stashed them.

Karen helped her count them.

"I have quite a few left. I'll get them over to Gila County and see if I can get a refund for them." Jean tallied the ribbons. "Hopefully we'll get our bins back from the police before next year."

Karen laughed. "Maybe. Who knows how long it will take? Have you heard anything else about Ina's murder?"

"I did. I spoke with Chief White early today. He told me he had gotten a warrant to search the K Seven bunk house and the ranch tool sheds. They found a ball peen hammer in a tool shed. He's had it in the lab, checking for blood and they found it."

"The murder weapon?"

"Apparently. Anyway, that and the finger prints on

my car from the tire slashing was all they needed to bring in Marlow. They found him at Analise's house. Why he was still there is beyond me. Anyway they brought him in and started questioning him and he blurt out everything. It was him, Analise and a young guy, Martin Johnson, the dark-haired man I saw having an argument with Analise. Martin was blackmailing her." Marlow confessed to attacking me. They picked up Johnson and after the man started talking, Nick came to pick up Analise but she was outside the truck. You know what happened after that.

"What a cow she is." Karen shook her head, then grinned. "Talking with the police chief first thing in the morning, huh?" She looked out of the corner of her eye at Jean as they put neatly stacked ribbons back in the box. "Chief White seems to have taken an interest in you."

Jean turned her head, eyebrows up. "You have got to be kidding. He was just filling in the details for me. The paper will have it all in a day or so. The man regards me as a total flake. You should have heard him yelling when he found out we went over to Analise's house."

"That's to be expected." Karen wiped the sweat from her forehead. They hadn't bothered to turn on the building fans. "You seem attracted to him."

"I was interested in the murder." Jean snorted. "What on earth do I want another man for? The last one was enough."

"Too soon, huh?"

Jean glared. "I am quite happy with my single state, thank you very much." She taped the cardboard box closed. "I come and go as I please. I cook when I feel like it. I have a lot of friends here already so I don't lack for company. Why would I want a guy around to mess all of that up?"

"Fine." Karen threw her hands up into the air. "Just sayin' it looked like you two were attracted."

"Nick White seems okay, but I'm not interested." Jean shook her head and picked up the box. "I'm taking this out to the car. I'll be back in a minute to finish closing this place up."

When she came back, Karen was sweeping up the last bits of dirt. "Find the dustpan, would ya?"

Jean found it next to the ladies room door. "Here you go." She squatted down to hold it while Karen swept the dirt in. "How about lunch?"

"I'd love it. Let's wash up here, then lock up."

"Fine by me." Jean looked around at the now barren building. Display cases were stacked neatly against the walls. The place echoed. "It's kind of sad, all empty like this."

Karen eyed her. "Yes. Yes it is."

The End

ABOUT THE AUTHOR

Connie Cockrell began writing in response to a challenge from her daughter in October 2011 and has been hooked ever since. Her books run the gamut from SciFi and Fantasy to Contemporary to Halloween and Christmas stories. She's published five novels and three collections of short stories and has been included in three different anthologies. Connie continues to write about whatever comes into her head.

Enjoyed Mystery at the Fair? Sign up to be notified of my next book at
http://conniesrandomthoughts.com/newsletter/

Discover other titles by Connie Cockrell at CreateSpace.com:
Recall: https://www.createspace.com/4270855
Halloween Tales: A Collection of Stories:
https://www.createspace.com/4270855
Christmas Tales: https://www.createspace.com/4530573
(Also available in Large Print)
Gulliver Station Stories: A New Start:
https://www.createspace.com/4649337 (Also available in Large Print)
The Brown Rain Series: First Encounter:
https://www.createspace.com/4980832
Lost Rainbows: https://www.createspace.com/5281034
Her books are available in print at most online retailers.

Her next book set in the Jean Hays series is called Mystery in the Woods. See the excerpt below.

If you'd like to know more, go to
http://www.conniesrandomthoughts. com or
https://www.facebook.com/ConniesRandomThoughts or
http://twitter.com/conniecockrell.

EXCERPT FROM THE JEAN HAYS SERIES: MYSTERY IN THE WOODS

Jean Hays was doing what she came to Arizona for, hiking. The fall colors in Arizona were muted, for the most part. Yellow dominated the central mountain's fall color scheme unless you hiked down into a canyon. Then, the hiker saw all the colors of an Eastern autumn day. Fallen leaves rustled underfoot and the smell was pure autumn—dusty, leafy, and woodsy. The sky was cloudless and she didn't have a name for the color, but it was only seen in October.

Her hiking partner was her best friend, Karen Carver. They'd first met when Jean joined the Hise County Fair board. Karen was a Superintendent at the fair in charge of Homemaking Arts. They'd hit it off right away. The Fair was over for the year. It was time to enjoy the countryside.

The stream bed they'd been following had a trickle of water in it. It caught the sky above and reflected that glorious blue. Red and yellow maple leaves floated along with the water. They were a little over two miles into the hike when they came to a small pool. Jean called a break. Karen slipped her pack from her back and pulled out a well used Girl Scout sit-upon.

"Looks like you've had that awhile," Jean said when she saw Karen spread it on a fallen tree trunk.

"I have." She sat down and pulled a granola bar from her pocket. "It was my daughter, Peggy's. It's still good, so I use it. I don't know if she even remembers I still have it." She looked at what Jean was pulling out of her pack. "What's that?"

"I cut up a foam floating mat to fit in the back of my pack. It's the perfect size, good protection from wet, cold," she examined a snag on the trunk and moved down a few inches, "and sharp things." She pulled a baggie of Sungold cherry tomatoes out of the pack. "The last of the garden cherries from my neighbor, want some?" Jean held out the bag.

Karen took four and popped one in her mouth. "Oh my, those are so good."

Jean pulled a water bottle from her pack's outside pocket and drank. Her eyes focused on something on the opposite side of the pool. "That doesn't look natural."

She walked around the pool and scrambled part way up the canyon's side to a tree. "It's a duffle bag," she called down to Karen. "It's a big duffle."

"Who'd carry a duffle bag on a hike?" Karen wondered.

Jean tugged at it. It came loose from where it had lodged against the tree and rolled down the slope. The rotten canvas, discolored and moldy, split open when it hit a rock. Jean slipped down the hill and looked inside. "Oh my, God." She danced away from the bag, back around the pool and stood panting beside Karen, now standing.

"What's wrong?"

Jean stared at the bag. "It's a body."

Mystery in the Woods is due out mid-June, 2016.

Made in the USA
Middletown, DE
11 May 2019